JAMES BALDWIN

Giovanni's Room

GREAT  LOVES

For Lucien

PENGUIN BOOKS

Published by the Penguin Group
Penguin Books Ltd, 80 Strand, London WC2R ORL, England
Penguin Books (USA) Inc., 375 Hudson Street, New York, New York 10014, USA
Penguin Group (Canada), 90 Eglinton Avenue East, Suite 700, Toronto, Ontario, Canada M4P 2Y3
(a division of Pearson Penguin Canada Inc.)
Penguin Ireland, 25 St Stephen's Green, Dublin 2, Ireland
(a division of Penguin Books Ltd)
Penguin Group (Australia), 250 Camberwell Road, Camberwell, Victoria 3124, Australia
(a division of Pearson Australia Group Pty Ltd)
Penguin Books India Pvt Ltd, 11 Community Centre, Panchsheel Park, New Delhi – 110 017, India
Penguin Group (NZ), 67 Apollo Drive, Rosedale, North Shore 0632, New Zealand
(a division of Pearson New Zealand Ltd)
Penguin Books (South Africa) (Pty) Ltd, 24 Sturdee Avenue,
Rosebank, Johannesburg 2196, South Africa

Penguin Books Ltd, Registered Offices: 80 Strand, London WC2R ORL, England

www.penguin.com

First published in the United States of America 1956
First published in Great Britain by Michael Joseph 1957
This edition published in Penguin Books 2007

2

Copyright 1956 James Baldwin
All rights reserved

Typeset by Rowland Phototypesetting Ltd, Bury St Edmunds, Suffolk
Printed in England by Clays Ltd, St Ives plc

978-0-141-03294-8

This edition produced for The Book People Ltd,
Hall Wood Avenue, Haydock, St Helens WA11 9UL

Giovanni's Room

James Baldwin (1924–1987) was born and educated in New York. *Go Tell It on the Mountain*, his first novel, was published in 1953. Evoking brilliantly his experiences as a boy preacher in Harlem, it was an immediate success and was followed by *Giovanni's Room*, which explores the theme of homosexual love in a sensitive and compelling way. *Another Country* (1963) created something of a literary explosion and was followed in 1964 by two non-fiction books, *Nobody knows My Name* and *Notes of a Native Son*, which contain several of the stories that brought him fame in America.

I am the man; I suffered, I was there.
                    – WHITMAN

Part One

I

I stand at the window of this great house in the south of France as night falls, the night which is leading me to the most terrible morning of my life. I have a drink in my hand, there is a bottle at my elbow. I watch my reflection in the darkening gleam of the window pane. My reflection is tall, perhaps rather like an arrow, my blond hair gleams. My face is like a face you have seen many times. My ancestors conquered a continent, pushing across death-laden plains, until they came to an ocean which faced away from Europe into a darker past.

I may be drunk by morning but that will not do any good. I shall take the train to Paris anyway. The train will be the same, the people, struggling for comfort and, even, dignity on the straight-backed, wooden, third-class seats will be the same, and I will be the same. We will ride through the same changing countryside northward, leaving behind the olive trees and the sea and all of the glory of the stormy southern sky, into the mist and rain of Paris. Someone will offer to share a sandwich with me, someone will offer me a sip of wine, someone will ask me for a match. People will be roaming the corridors outside, looking out of windows, looking in at us. At each stop, recruits in their baggy brown uniforms and colored hats will open the compartment door to ask *Complet?* We will all nod Yes, like conspirators, smiling faintly at each other as they continue through the train. Two or three of them will end up before our compartment door, shouting at each other in their heavy, ribald voices, smoking their dreadful army cigarettes. There will be a girl sitting opposite me who will wonder why I have not been flirting with her, who will be set on edge by the presence of the recruits. It will all be the same, only I will be stiller.

And the countryside is still tonight, this countryside reflected through my image in the pane. This house is just outside a small

3

summer resort – which is still empty, the season has not yet begun. It is on a small hill, one can look down on the lights of the town and hear the thud of the sea. My girl, Hella, and I rented it in Paris, from photographs, some months ago. Now she has been gone a week. She is on the high seas now, on her way back to America.

I can see her, very elegant, tense, and glittering, surrounded by the light which fills the salon of the ocean liner, drinking rather too fast, and laughing, and watching the men. That was how I met her, in a bar in St. Germain des Pres, she was drinking and watching, and that was why I liked her, I thought she would be fun to have fun with. That was how it began, that was all it meant to me; I am not sure now, in spite of everything, that it ever really meant more than that to me. And I don't think it ever really meant more than that to her – at least not until she made that trip to Spain and, finding herself there, alone, began to wonder, perhaps, if a lifetime of drinking and watching men was exactly what she wanted. But it was too late by that time. I was already with Giovanni. I had asked her to marry me before she went away to Spain; and she laughed and I laughed but that, somehow, all the same, made it more serious for me, and I persisted; and then she said she would have to go away and think about it. And the very last night she was here, the very last time I saw her, as she was packing her bag, I told her that I had loved her once and I made myself believe it. But I wonder if I had. I was thinking, no doubt, of our nights in bed, of the peculiar innocence and confidence which will never come again which had made those nights so delightful, so unrelated to past, present, or anything to come, so unrelated, finally, to my life since it was not necessary for me to take any but the most mechanical responsibility for them. And these nights were being acted out under a foreign sky, with no-one to watch, no penalties attached – it was this last fact which was our undoing, for nothing is more unbearable, once one has it, than freedom. I suppose this was why I asked her to marry me: to give myself something to be moored to. Perhaps this was why, in Spain, she decided that she wanted to marry me. But people can't, unhappily, invent their mooring posts, their lovers and their friends, anymore than they can invent their parents. Life gives these and also takes them away and the great difficulty is to say Yes to life.

I was thinking, when I told Hella that I had loved her, of those days before anything awful, irrevocable, had happened to me, when an affair was nothing more than an affair. Now, from this night, this coming morning, no matter how many beds I find myself in between now and my final bed, I shall never be able to have any more of those boyish, zestful affairs – which are, really, when one thinks of it, a kind of higher, or, anyway, more pretentious masturbation. People are too various to be treated so lightly. I am too various to be trusted. If this were not so I would not be alone in this house tonight. Hella would not be on the high seas. And Giovanni would not be about to perish, sometime between this night and this morning, on the guillotine.

I repent now – for all the good it does – one particular lie among the many lies I've told, told, lived, and believed. This is the lie which I told to Giovanni, but never succeeded in making him believe, that I had never slept with a boy before. I had. I had decided that I never would again. There is something fantastic in the spectacle I now present to myself of having run so far, so hard, across the ocean even, only to find myself brought up short once more before the bulldog in my own backyard – the yard, in the meantime, having grown smaller and the bulldog bigger.

I have not thought of that boy – Joey – for many years; but I see him quite clearly tonight. It was several years ago, I was still in my teens, he was about my age, give or take a year. He was a very nice boy, too, very quick and dark, and always laughing. For a while he was my best friend. Later, the idea that such a person *could* have been my best friend was proof of some horrifying taint in me. So I forgot him. But I see him very well tonight.

It was in the summer, there was no school. His parents had gone someplace for the weekend and I was spending the weekend at his house, which was near Coney Island, in Brooklyn. We lived in Brooklyn too, in those days, but in a better neighborhood than

Joey's. I think we had been lying around the beach, swimming a little and watching the near-naked girls pass, whistling at them, and laughing. I am sure that if any of the girls we whistled at that day had shown any signs of responding the ocean would not have been deep enough to drown our shame and terror. But the girls, no doubt, had some intimation of this, possibly from the way we whistled, and they ignored us. As the sun was setting we started up the boardwalk towards his house, with our wet bathing trunks on under our trousers.

And I think it began in the shower. I know that I felt something – as we were horsing around in that small, steamy room, stinging each other with wet towels – which I had not felt before, which mysteriously, and yet aimlessly, included him. I remember in myself a heavy reluctance to get dressed: I blamed it on the heat. But we did get dressed, sort of, and we ate cold things out of his icebox and drank a lot of beer. We must have gone to the movies. I can't think of any other reason for our going out and I remember walking down the dark, tropical Brooklyn streets with heat coming up from the pavements and banging from the walls of houses with enough force to kill a man, with all the world's grownups, it seemed, sitting shrill and dishevelled on the stoops and all the world's children on the sidewalks or in the gutters hanging from fire-escapes, with my arm around Joey's shoulder. I was proud, I think, because his head came just below my ear. We were walking along and Joey was making dirty wisecracks and we were laughing. Odd to remember, for the first time in so long, how good I felt that night, how fond of Joey.

When we came back along those streets it was quiet; we were quiet too. We were very quiet in the apartment and sleepily got undressed in Joey's bedroom and went to bed. I fell asleep – for quite awhile, I think. But I woke up to find the light on and Joey examining the pillow with great, ferocious care.

'What's the matter?'

'I think a bedbug bit me.'

'You slob. You got bedbugs?'

'I think one bit me.'

'You ever have a bedbug bite you before?'

'No.'

'Well, go back to sleep. You're dreaming.'

He looked at me with his mouth open and his dark eyes very big. It was as though he had just discovered that I was an expert on bedbugs. I laughed and grabbed his head as I had done God knows how many times before, when I was playing with him or when he had annoyed me. But this time when I touched him something happened in him and in me which made this touch different from any touch either of us had ever known. And he did not resist, as he usually did, but lay where I had pulled him, against my chest. And I realized that my heart was beating in an awful way and that Joey was trembling against me and the light in the room was very bright and hot. I started to move and to make some kind of joke but Joey mumbled something and I put my head down to hear. Joey raised his head as I lowered mine and we kissed, as it were, by accident. Then, for the first time in my life, I was really aware of another person's body, of another person's smell. We had our arms around each other. It was like holding in my hand some rare, exhausted, nearly doomed bird which I had miraculously happened to find. I was very frightened, I am sure he was frightened too, and we shut our eyes. To remember it so clearly, so painfully tonight tells me that I have never for an instant truly forgotten it. I feel in myself now a faint, dreadful stirring of what so overwhelmingly stirred in me then. Great thirsty heat, and trembling, and tenderness so painful I thought my heart would burst. But out of this astounding intolerable pain came joy, we gave each other joy that night. It seemed, then, that a lifetime would not be long enough for me to act with Joey the act of love.

But that lifetime was short, was bounded by that night – it ended in the morning. I awoke while Joey was still sleeping, curled like a baby on his side, toward me. He looked like a baby, his mouth half open, his cheek flushed, his curly hair darkening the pillow and half hiding his damp round forehead and his long eyelashes glinting slightly in the summer sun. We were both naked and the sheet we had used as a cover was tangled around our feet. Joey's body was

7

brown, was sweaty, the most beautiful creation I have ever seen till then. I would have touched him to wake him up but something stopped me. I was suddenly afraid. Perhaps it was because he looked so innocent lying there, with such perfect trust; perhaps it was because he was so much smaller than me; my own body suddenly seemed gross and crushing and the desire which was rising in me seemed monstrous. But, above all, I was suddenly afraid. It was borne in on me: *But Joey is a boy*, I saw suddenly the power in his thighs, in his arms, and in his loosely curled fists. The power and the promise and the mystery of that body made me suddenly afraid. That body suddenly seemed the black opening of a cavern in which I would be tortured till madness came, in which I would lose my manhood. Precisely, I wanted to know that mystery and feel that power and have that promise fulfilled through me. The sweat on my back grew cold. I was ashamed. The very bed, in its sweet disorder, testified to vileness. I wondered what Joey's mother would say when she saw the sheets. Then I thought of my father, who had no one in the world but me, my mother having died when I was little. A cavern opened in my mind, black, full of rumor, suggestion, of half-heard, half-forgotten, half-understood stories, full of dirty words. I thought I saw my future in that cavern. I was afraid. I could have cried, cried for shame and terror, cried for not understanding how this could have happened to me, how this could have happened *in* me. And I made my decision. I got out of bed and took a shower and was dressed and had breakfast ready when Joey woke up.

I did not tell him my decision, that would have broken my will. I did not wait to have breakfast with him but only drank some coffee and made an excuse to go home. I knew the excuse did not fool Joey; but he did not know how to protest or insist; he did not know that this was all he needed to have done. Then I, who had seen him that summer nearly every day till then, no longer went to see him. He did not come to see me. I would have been very happy to see him if he had, but the manner of my leavetaking had begun a constriction which neither of us knew how to arrest. When I finally did see him, more or less by accident, near the end of the summer, I made up a long and totally untrue story about a girl I was going with and when school began again I picked up with a rougher, older crowd and was very nasty to Joey. And the sadder this made him, the nastier I became. He moved away at last, out of the neighborhood, away from our school, and I never saw him again.

I began, perhaps, to be lonely that summer and began, that summer, the flight which has brought me to this darkening window.

And yet – when one begins to search for the crucial, the definitive moment, the moment which changed all others, one finds oneself pressing, in great pain, through a maze of false signals and abruptly locking doors. My flight may, indeed, have begun that summer – which does not tell me where to find the germ of the dilemma which resolved itself, that summer, into flight. Of course, it is somewhere before me, locked in that reflection I am watching in the window as the night comes down outside. It is trapped in the room with me, always has been, and always will be, and it is yet more foreign to me than those foreign hills outside.

We lived in Brooklyn then, as I say; we had also lived in San Francisco, where I was born, and where my mother lies buried, and we lived for awhile in Seattle, and then in New York – for me, New York is Manhattan. Later on, then, we moved from Brooklyn back to New York and by the time I came to France my father and his new wife had graduated to Connecticut. I had long been on my own by then, of course, and had been living in an apartment in the east sixties.

We, in the days when I was growing up, were my father and his unmarried sister and myself. My mother had been carried to the graveyard when I was five. I scarcely remember her at all, yet she figured in my nightmares, blind with worms, her hair as dry as metal and brittle as a twig, straining to press me against her body; that body so putrescent, so sickening soft, that it opened, as I clawed and cried, into a breach so enormous as to swallow me alive. But when my father or my aunt came rushing into my room to find out what had frightened me I did not dare describe this dream, which seemed disloyal to my mother. I said that I had dreamed

9

about a graveyard. They concluded that the death of my mother had had this unsettling effect on my imagination and perhaps they thought that I was grieving for her. And I may have been, but if that is so, then I am grieving still.

My father and my aunt got on very badly and, without ever knowing how or why I felt it, I felt that their long battle had everything to do with my dead mother. I remember when I was very young how, in the big living room of the house in San Francisco, my mother's photograph, which stood all by itself on the mantelpiece, seemed to rule the room. It was as though her photograph proved how her spirit dominated that air and controlled us all. I remember the shadows gathering in the far corners of that room, in which I never felt at home, and my father washed in the gold light which spilled down on him from the tall lamp which stood beside his easy chair. He would be reading his newspaper, hidden from me behind his newspaper, so that, desperate to conquer his attention, I some-times so annoyed him that our duel ended with me being carried from the room in tears. Or I remember him sitting bent forward, his elbows on his knees, staring toward the great window which held back the inky night. I used to wonder what he was thinking. In the eye of my memory he always wears a grey, sleeveless sweater and he had loosened his tie, and his sandy hair falls forward over a square, ruddy face. He was one of those people who, quick to laugh, are slow to anger; so that their anger, when it comes, is all the more impressive, seeming to leap from some unsuspected crevice like a fire which will bring the whole house down.

And his sister, Ellen, a little older than he, a little darker, always over-dressed, over made-up, with a face and figure beginning to harden, and with too much jewelry everywhere, clanging and bang-ing in the light, sits on the sofa, reading; she read a lot, all the new books, and she used to go to the movies a great deal. Or she knits. It seems to me that she was always carrying a great bag full of dangerous-looking knitting needles, or a book, or both. And I don't know what she knitted, though I suppose she must, at least occasionally, have knitted something for my father, or me. But I don't remember it, any more than I remember the books she read.

It might always have been the same book and she might have been working on the same scarf, or sweater, or God knows what, all the years I knew her. Sometimes she and my father played cards – this was rare; sometimes they talked together in friendly, teasing tones, but this was dangerous. Their banter nearly always ended in a fight. Sometimes there was company and I was often allowed to watch them drink their cocktails. Then my father was at his best, boyish and expansive, moving about through the crowded room with a glass in his hand, refilling people's drinks, laughing a lot, handling all the men as though they were his brothers, and flirting with the women. Or no, not flirting with them, strutting like a cock before them. Ellen always seemed to be watching him as though she were afraid he would do something awful, watched him and watched the women and, yes, she flirted with the men in a strange, nerve-wracking kind of way. There she was, dressed, as they say, to kill, with her mouth redder than any blood, dressed in something which was either the wrong color, or too tight, or too young, the cocktail glass in her hand threatening, at any instant, to be reduced to shards, to splinters, and that voice going on and on like a razor blade on glass. When I was a little boy and I watched her in company, she frightened me.

But no matter what was happening in that room, my mother was watching it. She looked out of the photograph frame, a pale, blonde woman, delicately put together, dark-eyed, and straight-browed, with a nervous, gentle mouth. But something about the way the eyes were set in the head and stared straight out, something very faintly sardonic and knowing in the set of the mouth suggested that, somewhere beneath this tense fragility was a strength as various as it was unyielding and, like my father's wrath, dangerous because it was so entirely unexpected. My father rarely spoke of her and when he did he covered, by some mysterious means, his face; he spoke of her only as my mother and, in fact, as he spoke of her, he might have been speaking of his own. Ellen spoke of my mother often, saying what a remarkable woman she had been but she made me uncomfortable. I felt that I had no right to be the son of such a mother.

Years later, when I had become a man, I tried to get my father to talk about my mother. But Ellen was dead, he was about to marry again. He spoke of my mother, then, as Ellen had spoken of her and he might, indeed, have been speaking of Ellen.

They had a fight one night when I was about thirteen. They had a great many fights, of course; but perhaps I remember this one so clearly because it seemed to be about me.

I was in bed upstairs, asleep. It was quite late. I was suddenly awakened by the sound of my father's footfalls on the walk beneath my window. I could tell by the sound and the rhythm that he was a little drunk and I remember that at that moment a certain disappointment, an unprecedented sorrow entered into me. I had seen him drunk many times and had never felt this way – on the contrary, my father sometimes had great charm when he was drunk – but that night I suddenly felt that there was something in it, in him, to be despised.

I heard him come in. Then, at once, I heard Ellen's voice.

'Aren't you in bed yet?' my father asked. He was trying to be pleasant and trying to avoid a scene, but there was no cordiality in his voice, only strain and exasperation.

'I thought,' said Ellen, coldly, 'that someone ought to tell you what you're doing to your son.'

'What I'm doing to my son?' And he was about to say something more, something awful; but he caught himself and only said, with a resigned, drunken, despairing calm: 'What are you talking about, Ellen?'

'Do you really think,' she asked – I was certain that she was standing in the center of the room, with her hands folded before her, standing very straight and still – 'that you're the kind of man he ought to be when he grows up?' And, as my father said nothing: 'He *is* growing up, you know.' And then, spitefully, 'Which is more than I can say for you.'

'Go to bed, Ellen,' said my father – sounding very weary.

I had the feeling, since they were talking about me, that I ought to go downstairs and tell Ellen that whatever was wrong between my father and myself we could work out between us without her help. And, perhaps – which seems odd – I felt that she was disrespectful of *me*. For I had certainly never said a word to her about my father.

I heard his heavy, uneven footfalls as he moved across the room, toward the stairs.

'Don't think,' said Ellen, 'that I don't know where you've been.'

'I've been out – drinking –' said my father, 'and now I'd like to get a little sleep. Do you mind?'

'You've been with that girl, Beatrice,' said Ellen. 'That's where you always are and that's where all your money goes and all your manhood and self-respect, too.'

She had succeeded in making him angry. He began to stammer. 'If you think – if you *think* – that I'm going to stand – stand – stand here – and argue with *you* about my private life – *my* private life! – if you think I'm going to argue with *you* about it, why, you're out of your mind.'

'I certainly don't care,' said Ellen, 'what you do with yourself. It isn't *you* I'm worried about. It's only that you're the only person who has any authority over David. I don't. And he hasn't got any mother. And he only listens to me when he thinks it pleases you. Do you really think it's a good idea for David to see you staggering home drunk all the time? And don't fool yourself,' she added, after a moment, in a voice thick with passion, 'don't fool yourself that he doesn't know where you're coming from, don't think he doesn't know about your women!'

She was wrong. I don't think I did know about them – or I had never thought about them. But from that evening, I thought about them all the time. I could scarcely ever face a woman without wondering whether or not my father had, in Ellen's phrase, been 'interfering' with her.

'I think it barely possible,' said my father, 'that David has a cleaner mind than yours.'

The silence, then, in which my father climbed the stairs was by far the worst silence my life had ever known. I was wondering what they were thinking – each of them. I wondered how they looked. I wondered what I would see when I saw them in the morning.

'And listen,' said my father suddenly, from the middle of the staircase, in a voice which frightened me, 'all I want for David is that he grow up to be a man. And when I say a man, Ellen, I don't mean a Sunday school teacher.'

'A man,' said Ellen, shortly, 'is not the same thing as a bull. Good-night.'

'Good-night,' he said, after a moment.

And I heard him stagger past my door.

From that time on, with the mysterious, cunning, and dreadful intensity of the very young, I despised my father and I hated Ellen. It is hard to say why. I don't know why. But it allowed all of Ellen's prophecies about me to come true. She had said that there would come a time when nothing and nobody would be able to rule me, not even my father. And that time certainly came.

It was after Joey. The incident with Joey had shaken me profoundly and its effect was to make me secretive and cruel. I could not discuss what had happened to me with anyone, I could not even admit it to myself; and, while I never thought about it, it remained, nevertheless, at the bottom of my mind, as still and as awful as a decomposing corpse. And it changed, it thickened, it soured the atmosphere of my mind. Soon it was I who came staggering home late at night, it was I who found Ellen waiting up for me, Ellen and I who wrangled night in and night out.

My father's attitude was that this was but an inevitable phase of my growing up and he affected to take it lightly. But beneath his jocular, boys-together air, he was at a loss, he was frightened. Perhaps he had supposed that my growing up would bring us closer together – whereas, now that he was trying to find out something about me, I was in full flight from him. I did not *want* him to know me. I did not want anyone to know me. And then, again, I was undergoing with my father what the very young inevitably undergo with their elders: I was beginning to judge him. And the very harshness of this judgment, which broke my heart, revealed, though I could not have said it then, how much I had loved him, how that love, along with my innocence, was dying.

My poor father was baffled and afraid. He was unable to believe that there could be anything seriously wrong between us. And this was not only because he would not then have known what to do about it; it was mainly because he would then have had to face the knowledge that he had left something, somewhere, undone, something of the utmost importance. And since neither of us had any idea of what this so significant omission could have been, and since we were forced to remain in tacit league against Ellen, we took refuge in being hearty with each other. We were not like father and son, my father sometimes proudly said, we were like buddies. I think my father sometimes actually believed this. I never did. I did not want to be his buddy, I wanted to be his son. What passed between us as masculine candor exhausted and appalled me. Fathers ought to avoid utter nakedness before their sons. I did not want to know – not, anyway, from his mouth – that his flesh was as unregenerate as my own. The knowledge did not make me feel more like his son – or buddy – it only made me feel like an interloper, and a frightened one at that. He thought we were alike. I did not want to think so. I did not want to think that my life would be like his, or that my mind would ever grow so pale, so without hard places and sharp, sheer drops. He wanted no distance between us, he wanted me to look on him as a man like myself. But I wanted the merciful distance of father and son, which would have permitted me to love him.

One night, drunk, with several other people on the way back from an out of town party, the car I was driving smashed up. It was entirely my fault. I was almost too drunk to walk and had no business driving; but the others did not know this, since I am one of those people who can look and sound sober while practically in a state of collapse. On a straight, level piece of highway something weird happened to all my reactions and the car sprang suddenly out of my control. And a telephone pole, foam white, came crying at me out of the pitch darkness; I heard screams and then a heavy, roaring, tearing sound. Then everything turned absolutely scarlet and then as bright as day and I went into a darkness I had never known before.

I must have begun to wake up as we were being moved to the

15

hospital. I dimly remember movement and voices, but they seemed very far away, they seemed to have nothing to do with me. Then, later, I woke up in a spot which seemed to be the very heart of winter, a high, white ceiling and white walls, and a hard, glacial window, bent, as it seemed, over me. I must have tried to rise, for I remember an awful roaring in my head, and then a weight on my chest and a huge face over me. And as this weight, this face, began to push me under again, I screamed for my mother. Then it was dark again.

When I came to myself at last, my father was standing over my bed. I knew he was there before I saw him, before my eyes focussed and I carefully turned my head. When he saw that I was awake, he carefully stepped closer to the bed, motioning me to be still. And he looked very old. I wanted to cry. For a moment we just stared at each other.

'How do you feel?' he whispered, finally.

It was when I tried to speak that I realized I was in pain and immediately I was frightened. He must have seen this in my eyes, for he said in a low voice, with a pained, a marvellous intensity, 'Don't worry, David. You're going to be alright. You're going to be alright.'

I still could not say anything. I simply watched his face.

'You kids were mighty lucky,' he said, trying to smile. 'You're the one got smashed up the most.'

'I was drunk,' I said at last. I wanted to tell him everything – but speaking was such agony.

'Don't you know,' he asked, with an air of extreme bafflement – for this was something he could allow himself to be baffled about – 'better than to go driving around like that when you're drunk? You know better than that,' he said, severely, and pursed his lips. 'Why you could all have been killed.' And his voice shook.

'I'm sorry,' I said, suddenly. 'I'm sorry.' I did not know how to say what it was I was sorry for.

'Don't be sorry,' he said. 'Just be careful next time.' He had been patting his handkerchief between his palms; now he opened this handkerchief and reached out and wiped my forehead. 'You're all I've got,' he said then, with a shy, pained grin. 'Be careful.'

'Daddy,' I said. And began to cry. And if speaking had been agony, this was worse and yet I could not stop.

And my father's face changed. It became terribly old and at the same time absolutely, helplessly young. I remember being absolutely astonished, at the still, cold center of the storm which was occurring in me, to realize that my father had been suffering, was suffering still.

'Don't cry,' he said, 'don't cry.' He stroked my forehead with that absurd handkerchief as though it possessed some healing charm. 'There's nothing to cry about. Everything's going to be all right.' He was almost weeping himself. 'There's nothing wrong, is there? I haven't done anything wrong, have I?' And all the time he was stroking my face with that handkerchief, smothering me.

'We were drunk,' I said. 'We were drunk.' For this seemed, somehow, to explain everything.

'Your aunt Ellen says it's my fault,' he said. 'She says I never raised you right.' He put away, thank heaven, that handkerchief, and weakly straightened his shoulders. 'You got nothing against me, have you? Tell me if you have?'

My tears began to dry, on my face and in my breast. 'No,' I said, 'no. Nothing. Honest.'

'I did the best I could,' he said. 'I really did the best I could.' I looked at him. And at last he grinned and said, 'You're going to be on your back for awhile but when you come home, while you're lying around the house, we'll talk, huh? and try to figure out what the hell we're going to do with you when you get on your feet. OK?'

'OK,' I said.

For I understood, at the bottom of my heart, that we had never talked, that now we never would. I understood that he must never know this. When I came home he talked with me about my future but I had made up my mind. I was not going to go to college. I was not going to remain in that house with him and Ellen. And I maneuvered my father so well that he actually began to believe that my finding a job and being on my own was the direct result of his advice and a tribute to the way he had raised me. Once I was out of the house, of course, it became much easier to deal with him and he never had any reason to feel shut out of my life for I was always able, when talking about it, to tell him what he wished to hear. And we got on quite well, really, for the vision I gave my father of my life was exactly the vision in which I myself most desperately needed to believe.

For I am – or I was – one of those people who pride themselves on their willpower, on their ability to make a decision and carry it through. This virtue, like most virtues, is ambiguity itself. People who believe that they are strong-willed and the masters of their destiny can only continue to believe this by becoming specialists in self-deception. Their decisions are not really decisions at all – a real decision makes one humble, one knows that it is at the mercy of more things than can be named – but elaborate systems of evasion, of illusion, designed to make themselves and the world appear to be what they and the world are not. This is certainly what my decision, made so long ago in Joey's bed, came to. I had decided to allow no room in the universe for something which shamed and frightened me. I succeeded very well – by not looking at the universe, by not looking at myself, by remaining, in effect, in constant motion. Even constant motion, of course, does not prevent an occasional mysterious drag, a drop, like an airplane hitting an air pocket. And there were a number of those, all drunken, all sordid, one very frightening such drop while I was in the Army which involved a fairy who was later court-martialed out. The panic his punishment caused in me was as close as I ever came to facing in myself the terrors I sometimes saw clouding another man's eyes.

What happened was that, all unconscious of what this ennui meant, I wearied of the motion, wearied of the joyless seas of alcohol, wearied of the blunt, bluff, hearty, and totally meaningless friendships, wearied of wandering through the forests of desperate women, wearied of the work which fed me only in the most brutally literal sense. Perhaps, as we say in America, I wanted to find myself. This is an interesting phrase, not current as far as I know in the language of any other people, which certainly does not mean what it says but betrays a nagging suspicion that something has been misplaced. I think now that if I had had any intimation that the self I was going to find would turn out to be only the same self from which I had spent so much time in flight, I would have stayed at home. But again, I think I knew, at the very bottom of my heart, exactly what I was doing when I took the boat for France.

2

I met Giovanni during my second year in Paris, when I had no money. On the morning of the evening that we met I had been turned out of my room. I did not owe an awful lot of money, only around six thousand francs, but Parisian hotel-keepers have a way of smelling poverty and then they do what anybody does who is aware of a bad smell, they throw whatever stinks outside.

My father had money in his account which belonged to me but he was very reluctant to send it because he wanted me to come home – to come home, as he said, and settle down, and whenever he said that I thought of the sediment at the bottom of a stagnant pond. I did not, then, know many people in Paris and Hella was in Spain. Most of the people I knew in Paris were, as Parisians sometimes put it, of *le milieu* and, while this milieu was certainly anxious enough to claim me, I was intent on proving, to them and to myself, that I was not of their company. I did this by being in their company a great deal and manifesting toward all of them a tolerance which placed me, I believe, above suspicion. I had written to friends for money, of course, but the Atlantic Ocean is deep and wide and money doesn't hurry from the other side.

So I went through my address book, sitting over a tepid coffee in a boulevard cafe, and decided to call up an old acquaintance who was always asking me to call, an aging, Belgian-born, American businessman, named Jacques. He had a big, comfortable apartment and lots of things to drink and lots of money. He was, as I knew he would be, surprised to hear from me and before the surprise and the charm wore off, giving him time to become wary, he had invited me for supper. He may have been cursing as he hung up, and reaching for his wallet but it was too late. Jacques is not too bad. Perhaps he is a fool and a coward but almost everybody is one or the other and most people are both. In some ways I liked him. He was silly but he was so lonely; anyway, I understand now that the contempt I felt for him involved my self-contempt. He could be unbelievably generous, he could be unspeakably stingy. Though he wanted to trust everybody, he was incapable of trusting a living soul; to make up for this, he threw his money away on people; inevitably, then, he was abused. Then he buttoned his wallet, locked his door, and retired into that strong self-pity which was, perhaps, the only thing he had which really belonged to him. I thought for a long while that he, with his big apartment, his well-meant promises, his whisky, his marijuana, his orgies, had helped to kill Giovanni. As, indeed, perhaps he had. But Jacques' hands are certainly no bloodier than mine.

I saw Jacques, as a matter of fact, just after Giovanni was sentenced. He was sitting bundled up in his greatcoat on the terrace of a cafe, drinking a *vin chaud*. He was alone on the terrace. He called me as I passed.

He did not look well, his face was mottled, his eyes, behind his glasses, were like the eyes of a dying man who looks everywhere for healing.

'You've heard,' he whispered, as I joined him, 'about Giovanni?'

I nodded yes. I remember the winter sun was shining and I felt as cold and distant as the sun.

'It's terrible, terrible, terrible,' Jacques moaned. 'Terrible.'

'Yes,' I said. I could not say anything more.

'I wonder why he did it,' Jacques pursued, 'why he didn't ask his friends to help him.' He looked at me. We both knew that the last time Giovanni had asked Jacques for money, Jacques had refused. I said nothing. 'They say he had started taking opium,' Jacques said, 'that he needed the money for opium. Did you hear that?'

I had heard it. It was a newspaper speculation which, however, I had reasons of my own for believing, remembering the extent of Giovanni's desperation, knowing how far this terror which was so vast that it had simply become a void had driven him. 'Me, I want to escape,' he had told me, '*je veuz m'evader* – this dirty world, this dirty body. I never wish to make love again with anything more than the body.'

Jacques waited for me to answer. I stared out into the street. I was beginning to think of Giovanni dying – where Giovanni had been there would be nothing, nothing forever.

'I hope it's not my fault,' Jacques said at last. 'I didn't give him the money. If I'd known – I would have given him everything I had.'

But we both knew this was not true.

'You two together,' Jacques suggested, 'you weren't happy together?'

'No,' I said. I stood up. 'It might have been better,' I said, 'if he'd stayed down there in that village of his in Italy and planted his olive trees and had a lot of children and beaten his wife. He used to love to sing,' I remembered suddenly, 'maybe he could have stayed down there and sung his life away and died in bed.'

Then Jacques said something that surprised me. People are full of surprises, even for themselves, if they have been stirred enough. 'Nobody can stay in the garden of Eden,' Jacques said. And then: 'I wonder why.'

I said nothing. I said goodbye and left him. Hella had long since returned from Spain and we were already arranging to rent this house and I had a date to meet her.

I have thought about Jacques' question since. The question is banal but one of the real troubles with living is that living is so banal. Everyone, after all, goes the same dark road – and the road has a trick of being most dark, most treacherous, when it seems most bright – and it's true that nobody stays in the garden of Eden. Jacques' garden was not the same as Giovanni's, of course. Jacques' garden was involved with football players and Giovanni's was involved with maidens – but that seems to have made so little difference. Perhaps everybody has a garden of Eden, I don't know; but they have scarcely seen their garden before they see the flaming sword. Then, perhaps, life only offers the choice of remembering the garden or forgetting it. Either, or: it takes strength to remember, it takes another kind of strength to forget, it takes a hero to do both. People who remember court madness through pain, the pain of the perpetually recurring death of their innocence; people who forget court another kind of madness, the madness of the denial of pain and the hatred of innocence; and the world is mostly divided between madmen who remember and madmen who forget. Heroes are rare.

Jacques had not wanted to have supper in his apartment because his cook had run away. His cooks were always running away. He was always getting young boys from the provinces, God knows how, to come up and be cooks; and they, of course, as soon as they were able to find their way around the capital, decided that cooking was the last thing they wanted to do. They usually ended up going back to the provinces, those, that is, who did not end up on the streets, or in jail, or in Indo-China.

I met him at a rather nice restaurant on the rue de Grenelle and arranged to borrow ten thousand francs from him before we had finished our aperitifs. He was in a good mood and I, of course, was in a good mood too, and this meant that we would end up drinking in Jacques' favorite bar, a noisy, crowded, ill-lit sort of tunnel, of dubious – or perhaps not dubious at all, of rather too emphatic – reputation. Every once in a while it was raided by the police, apparently with the connivance of Guillaume, the *patron*, who always managed, on the particular evening, to warn his favorite customers that if they were not armed with identification papers they might be better off elsewhere.

I remember that the bar, that night, was more than ordinarily crowded and noisy. All of the habitués were there and many strangers, some looking, some just staring. There were three or four very chic Parisian ladies sitting at a table with their gigolos or their lovers or perhaps simply their country cousins, God knows; the ladies seemed extremely animated, their males seemed rather stiff; the ladies seemed to be doing most of the drinking. There were the usual paunchy, bespectacled gentlemen with avid, sometimes despairing eyes, the usual, knife-blade lean, tight-trousered boys. One could never be sure, as concerns these latter, whether they were after money or blood or love. They moved about the bar incessantly, cadging cigarettes and drinks, with something behind their eyes at once terribly vulnerable and terribly hard. There were, of course, *les folles*, always dressed in the most improbable combinations, screaming like parrots the details of their latest love-affairs – their love-affairs always seemed to be hilarious. Occasionally one would swoop in, quite late in the evening, to convey the news that he – but they always called each other 'she' – had just spent time with a celebrated movie star, or boxer. Then all of the others closed in on this newcomer and they looked like a peacock garden and sounded like a barnyard. I always found it difficult to believe that they ever went to bed with anybody for a man who wanted a woman would certainly have rather had a real one and a man who wanted a man would certainly not want one of *them*. Perhaps, indeed, that was why they screamed so loud. There was the boy who worked all day, it was said, in the post-office, who came out at night wearing makeup and earrings and with his heavy blond hair piled high. Sometimes he actually wore a skirt and high heels. He usually stood alone unless Guillaume walked over to tease him. People said that he was very nice but I confess that his utter grotesqueness made me uneasy; perhaps in the same way that the sight of monkeys eating their own excrement turns some people's stomachs. They might not mind so much if monkeys did not – so grotesquely – resemble human beings.

This bar was practically in my *quartier* and I had many times had breakfast in the nearby working man's cafe to which all the nightbirds of the neighborhood retired when the bars closed. Sometimes I was with Hella, sometimes I was alone. And I had been in this bar, too, two or three times; once very drunk. I had been accused of causing a minor sensation by flirting with a soldier. My memory of that night was, happily, very dim, and I took the attitude that no matter how drunk I may have been I could not possibly have done such a thing. But my face was known and I had the feeling that people were taking bets about me. Or, it was as though they were the elders of some strange and austere holy order and were watching me in order to discover, by means of signs I made but which only they could read, whether or not I had a true vocation.

Jacques was aware, I was aware, as we pushed our way to the bar – it was like moving into the field of a magnet or like approaching a small circle of heat – of the presence of a new barman. He stood, insolent and dark and leonine, his elbow leaning on the cash-register, his fingers playing with his chin, looking out at the crowd. It was as though his station was a promontory and we were the sea.

Jacques was immediately attracted. I felt him, so to speak, preparing himself for conquest. I felt the necessity for tolerance.

'I'm sure,' I said, 'that you'll want to get to know the barman. So I'll vanish any time you like.'

There was, in this tolerance of mine, a fund, by no means meagre, of malicious knowledge – I had drawn on it when I called him up to borrow money. I knew that Jacques could only hope to conquer the boy before us if the boy was in effect, for sale; and if he stood with such arrogance on an auction block he could certainly find bidders richer and more attractive than Jacques. I knew that Jacques knew this. I knew something else: that Jacques' vaunted affection for me was involved with desire, the desire, in fact, to be rid of me, to be able, soon, to despise me as he now despised that army of boys who had come, without love, to his bed. I held my own against this desire by pretending that Jacques and I were friends, by forcing Jacques, on pain of humiliation, to pretend this. I pretended not to see, although I exploited it, the lust not quite sleeping in his bright, bitter eyes and, by means of the rough, male candor with which I conveyed to him his case was hopeless, I compelled him, endlessly, to hope. And I knew, finally, that in bars such as these I was Jacques' protection. As long as I was there the world could see and he could believe that he was out with me, his friend, he was not there out of desperation, he was not at the mercy of whatever adventurer chance, cruelty, or the laws of actual and emotional poverty might throw his way.

'You stay right here,' said Jacques. 'I'll look at him from time to time and talk to you and that way I'll save money – and stay happy, too.'

'I wonder where Guillaume found him,' I said.

For he was so exactly the kind of boy that Guillaume always dreamed of that it scarcely seemed possible that Guillaume could have found him.

'What will you have?' he now asked us. His tone conveyed that, though he spoke no English, he knew that we had been speaking about him and hoped we were through.

'*Une fine a l'eau*,' I said; and '*un cognac sec*,' said Jacques, both speaking too quickly, so that I blushed and realized by a faint merriment on Giovanni's face as he served us that he had seen it.

Jacques, wilfully misinterpreting Giovanni's nuance of a smile, made of it an opportunity. 'You're new here?' he asked in English.

Giovanni almost certainly understood the question but it suited him better to look blankly from Jacques to me and then back again at Jacques. Jacques translated his question.

Giovanni shrugged. 'I have been here a month,' he said.

I knew where the conversation was going and I kept my eyes down and sipped my drink.

'It must,' Jacques suggested, with a sort of bludgeoning insistence on the light touch, 'seem very strange to you.'

'Strange?' asked Giovanni. 'Why?'

And Jacques giggled. I was suddenly ashamed that I was with him. 'All these men' – and I knew that voice, breathless, insinuating, high as no girl's had ever been, and hot, suggesting, somehow, the absolutely motionless, deadly heat which hangs over swamp ground in July – 'all these men,' he gasped, 'and so few women. Doesn't that seem strange to you?'

'Ah,' said Giovanni, and turned away to serve another customer, 'no doubt the women are waiting at home.'

'I'm sure one's waiting for you,' insisted Jacques, to which Giovanni did not respond.

'Well. That didn't take long,' said Jacques, half to me, half to the space which had just held Giovanni. 'Aren't you glad you stayed? You've got me all to yourself.'

'Oh, you're handling it all wrong,' I said. 'He's mad for you. He just doesn't want to seem too anxious. Order him a drink. Find out where he likes to buy his clothes. Tell him about that cunning little Alfa Romeo you're just dying to give away to some deserving bartender.'

'*Very* funny,' said Jacques.

'Well,' I said, 'faint heart never won fair athlete, that's for sure.'

'Anyway, I'm sure he sleeps with girls. They always do, you know.'

'I've heard about boys who do that. Nasty little beasts.'

We stood in silence for awhile.

'Why don't *you* invite him to have a drink with us?' Jacques suggested.

I looked at him.

'Why don't *I*? Well, you may find this hard to believe, but, actually, I'm sort of queer for girls myself. If that was his sister looking so good, I'd invite *her* to have a drink with us. I don't spend money on men.'

I could see Jacques struggling not to say that I didn't have any objection to allowing men to spend money on *me*; I watched his brief struggle with a slight smile, for I knew he couldn't say it; then he said, with that cheery, brave smile of his:

'I was not suggesting that you jeopardize, even for a moment, that' – he paused – 'that *immaculate* manhood which is your pride and joy. I only suggested that *you* invite him because he will almost certainly refuse if *I* invite him.'

'But man,' I said, grinning, 'think of the confusion. He'll think that *I'm* the one who's lusting for his body. How do we get out of that?'

'If there should be any confusion,' said Jacques, with dignity, 'I will be happy to clear it up.'

We measured each other for a moment. Then I laughed. 'Wait till he comes back this way. I hope he orders a magnum of the most expensive champagne in France.'

I turned, leaning on the bar. I felt somehow, elated. Jacques, beside me, was very quiet, suddenly very frail and old, and I felt a quick, sharp, rather frightened pity for him. Giovanni had been out on the floor, serving the people at tables, and he now returned with a rather grim smile on his face, carrying a loaded tray.

'Maybe,' I said, 'it would look better if our glasses were empty.'

We finished our drinks. I set down my glass.

'Barman?' I called.

James Baldwin

'The same?'

'Yes.' He started to turn away. 'Barman,' I said, quickly, 'we would like to offer you a drink, if we may.'

'*Eh, bien!*' said a voice behind us, '*cest fort ça!* Not only have you finally – thank heaven! – corrupted this great American football player, you use him now to corrupt *my* barman. *Vraiment, Jacques! At your age!*'

It was Guillaume standing behind us, grinning like a movie star, and waving that long white handkerchief which he was never, in the bar at any rate, to be seen without. Jacques turned, hugely delighted to be accused of such rare seductiveness, and he and Guillaume fell into each other's arms like old theatrical sisters.

'*Eh bien, ma cheri, comment vas tu?* I have not seen you for a long time.'

'But I have been awfully busy,' said Jacques.

'I don't doubt it! Aren't you ashamed, *veille folle?*'

'*Et toi?* You certainly don't seem to have been wasting your time.'

And Jacques threw a delighted look in the direction of Giovanni, rather as though Giovanni were a valuable race horse or a rare bit of china. Guillaume followed the look and his voice dropped.

'*Ah, ça, mon cher, c'est strictement du* business, *comprendstu?*'

They moved a little away. This left me surrounded, abruptly, with an awful silence. At last I raised my eyes and looked at Giovanni, who was watching me.

'I think you offered me a drink,' he said.

'Yes,' I said. 'I offered you a drink.'

'I drink no alcohol while I work, but I will take a Coca-Cola.' He picked up my glass. 'And for you – it is the same?'

'The same.' I realized I was quite happy to be talking with him and this realization made me shy. And I felt menaced since Jacques was no longer at my side. Then I realized that I would have to pay, for this round anyway; it was impossible to tug Jacques' sleeve for the money as though I were his ward. I coughed and put my ten thousand franc note on the bar.

'You are rich,' said Giovanni, and set my drink before me.

'But no. No. I simply have no change.'

28

He grinned. I could not tell whether he grinned because he thought I was lying or because he knew I was telling the truth. In silence he took the bill and rang it up and carefully counted out my change on the bar before me. Then he filled his glass and went back to his original position at the cash-register. I felt a tightening in my chest.

'*A la votre*,' he said.

'*A la votre*.' We drank.

'You are an American?' he asked at last.

'Yes,' I said. 'From New York.'

'Ah! I am told that New York is very beautiful. Is it more beautiful than Paris?'

'Oh, no,' I said, '*no* city is more beautiful than Paris –'

'It seems the very suggestion that one *could* be is enough to make you very angry,' grinned Giovanni. 'Forgive me. I was not trying to be heretical.' Then, more soberly and as though to appease me, 'You must like Paris very much.'

'I like New York, too,' I said, uncomfortably aware that my voice had a defensive ring, 'but New York is very beautiful in a very different way.'

He frowned. 'In what way?'

'No one,' I said, 'who has never seen it can possibly imagine it. It's very high and new and electric – exciting.' I paused. 'It's hard to describe. It's very – twentieth century.'

'You find that Paris is *not* of this century?' he asked with a smile.

His smile made me feel a little foolish. 'Well,' I said, 'Paris is *old*, is many centuries. You feel, in Paris, all the time gone by. That isn't what you feel in New York –' He was smiling. I stopped.

'What do you feel in New York?' he asked.

'Perhaps you feel,' I told him, 'all the time to come. There's such power there, everything is in such movement. You can't help wondering – *I* can't help wondering – what it will all be like – many years from now.'

'Many years from now? When we are dead and New York is old?'

'Yes,' I said. 'When everyone is tired, when the world – for Americans – is not so new.'

'I don't see why the world is so new for Americans,' said Giovanni. 'After all, you are all merely emigrants. And you did not leave Europe so very long ago.'

'The ocean is very wide,' I said. 'We have led different lives than you, things have happened to us there which have never happened here. Surely you can understand that this would make us a different people?'

'Ah! If it had only made you a different people!' he laughed. 'But it seems to have turned you into another species. You are not, are you, on another planet? For I suppose that would explain everything.'

'I admit,' I said with some heat – for I do not like to be laughed at – 'that we may sometimes give the impression that we think we are. But we are not on another planet, no. And neither, my friend, are you.'

He grinned again. 'I will not,' he said, 'argue that most unlucky fact.'

We were silent for a moment. Giovanni moved to serve several people at either end of the bar. Guillaume and Jacques were still talking. Guillaume seemed to be recounting one of his interminable anecdotes, anecdotes which invariably pivoted on the hazards of business or the hazards of love, and Jacques' mouth was stretched in a rather painful grin. I knew that he was dying to get back to the bar.

Giovanni placed himself before me again and began wiping the bar with a damp cloth. 'The Americans are funny. You have a funny sense of time – or perhaps you have no sense of time at all, I can't tell. Time always sounds like a parade *chez vous* – a *triumphant* parade, like armies with banners entering a town. As though, with enough time, and that would not need to be so very much for Americans, *n'est-ce pas?*' and he smiled, giving me a mocking look, but I said nothing. 'Well then,' he continued, 'as though with enough time and all that fearful energy and virtue you people have, everything will be settled, solved, put in its place. And when I say everything,' he added, grimly, 'I mean all the serious, dreadful things, like pain and death and love, in which you Americans do not believe.'

'What makes you think we don't? And what do you believe?'

'I don't believe in this nonsense about time. Time is just common, it's like water for a fish. Everybody's in this water, nobody gets out of it, or if he does the same thing happens to him that happens to the fish, he dies. And you know what happens in this water, time? The big fish eat the little fish. That's all. The big fish eat the little fish and the ocean doesn't care.'

'Oh, please,' I said. 'I don't believe *that*. Time's not water and we're not fish and you can choose to be eaten and also not to eat – not to eat,' I added quickly, turning a little red before his delighted and sardonic smile, 'the little fish, of course.'

'To choose!' cried Giovanni, turning his face away from me and speaking, it appeared, to an invisible ally who had been eavesdropping on this conversation all along. 'To *choose*!' He turned to me again. 'Ah, you are really an American. *J'adore votre enthousiasme!*'

'I adore yours,' I said, politely, 'though it seems to be a blacker brand than mine.'

'Anyway,' he said mildly, 'I don't see what you can do with little fish except eat them. What else are they good for?'

'In my country,' I said, feeling a subtle war within me as I said it, 'the little fish seem to have gotten together and are nibbling at the body of the whale.'

'That will not make them whales,' said Giovanni. 'The only result of all that nibbling will be that there will no longer be any grandeur anywhere, not even at the bottom of the sea.'

'Is *that* what you have against us? That we're not grand?'

He smiled – smiled like someone who, faced with the total inadequacy of the opposition, is prepared to drop the argument. '*Peut-être.*'

'You people are impossible,' I said. 'You're the ones who killed grandeur off, right here in this city, with paving stones. Talk about little fish –!' He was grinning. I stopped.

'Don't stop,' he said, still grinning. 'I am listening.'

I finished my drink. 'You people dumped all this *merde* on us,' I said, sullenly, 'and now you say we're barbaric because we stink.'

My sullenness delighted him. 'You're charming,' he said. 'Do you always speak like this?'

31

'No,' I said, and looked down. 'Almost never.'

There was something in him of the coquette. 'I am flattered then,' he said, with a sudden, disconcerting gravity, which contained, nevertheless, the very faintest hint of mockery.

'And you,' I said, finally, 'have you been here long? Do you like Paris?'

He hesitated a moment and then grinned, suddenly looking rather boyish and shy. 'It's cold in the winter,' he said. 'I don't like that. And Parisians – I do not find them so very friendly, do you?' He did not wait for my answer. 'They are not like the people I knew when I was younger. In Italy we are friendly, we dance and sing and make love – but these people,' and he looked out over the bar, and then at me, and finished his Coca-Cola, 'these people, they are cold, I do not understand them.'

'But the French say,' I teased, 'that the Italians are too fluid, too volatile, have no sense of measure –'

'Measure!' cried Giovanni, 'ah, these people and their measure! They measure the gram, the centimetre, these people, and they keep piling all the little scraps they save, one on top of the other, year in and year out, all in the stocking or under the bed – and what do they get out of all this measure? A country which is falling to pieces, measure by measure, before their eyes. Measure. I do not like to offend your ears by saying all the things I am sure these people measure before they permit themselves any act whatever. May I offer you a drink now,' he asked suddenly, 'before the old man comes back? Who is he? Is he your uncle?'

I did not know whether the world 'uncle' was being used euphemistically or not. I felt a very urgent desire to make my position clear but I did not know how to go about it. I laughed. 'No,' I said, 'he is not my uncle. He is just somebody I know.'

Giovanni looked at me. And this look made me feel that no one in my life had ever looked at me directly before. 'I hope he is not very dear to you,' he said, with a smile, 'because I think he is silly. Not a bad man, you understand – just a little silly.'

'Perhaps,' I said, and at once felt like a traitor. 'He's not bad,' I added quickly, 'he's really a pretty nice guy.' That's not true, either, I thought, he's far from being a nice guy. 'Anyway,' I said, 'he's certainly not very dear to me,' and felt again, at once, this strange tightening in my chest and wondered at the sound of my voice.

Carefully now, Giovanni poured my drink. '*Vive l'amerique,*' he said.

'Thank you,' I said, and lifted my glass, '*vive le vieux continent.*'

We were silent for a moment.

'Do you come in here often?' asked Giovanni suddenly.

'No,' I said, 'not very often.'

'But you will come,' he teased, with a wonderful, mocking light on his face, 'more often *now*?'

I stammered: 'Why?'

'Ah!' cried Giovanni. 'Don't you know when you have made a friend?'

I knew I must look foolish and that my question was foolish too: 'So soon?'

'Why no,' he said, reasonably, and looked at his watch, 'we can wait another hour if you like. We can become friends then. Or we can wait until closing time. We can become friends *then*. Or we can wait until tomorrow, only that means that you must come in here tomorrow and perhaps you have something else to do.' He put his watch away and leaned both elbows on the bar. 'Tell me,' he said, 'what is this thing about time? Why is it better to be late than early? People are always saying, we must wait, we must wait. What are they waiting for?'

'Well,' I said, feeling myself being led by Giovanni into deep and dangerous water, 'I guess people wait in order to make sure of what they feel.'

'In order to make *sure*!' He turned again to that invisible ally and laughed again. I was beginning, perhaps, to find his phantom a little unnerving but the sound of his laughter in that airless tunnel was the most incredible sound. 'It's clear that you are a true philosopher.' He pointed a finger at my heart. 'And when you have waited – has it made you sure?'

For this I could simply summon no answer. From the dark,

crowded center of the bar someone called '*Garçon!*' and he moved away from me, smiling. 'You can wait now. And tell me how sure you have become when I return.'

And he took his round metal tray and moved out into the crowd. I watched him as he moved. And then I watched their faces, watching him. And then I was afraid. I knew that they were watching, had been watching both of us. They knew that they had witnessed a beginning and now they would not cease to watch until they saw the end. It had taken some time but the tables had been turned, now I was in the zoo, and they were watching.

I stood at the bar for quite a while alone, for Jacques had escaped from Guillaume but was now involved, poor man, with two of the knife-blade boys. Giovanni came back for an instant and winked.

'Are you sure?'

'You win. You're the philosopher.'

'Oh, you must wait some more. You do not yet know me well enough to say such a thing.'

And he filled his tray and disappeared again.

Now someone whom I had never seen before came out of the shadows toward me. It looked like a mummy or a zombie – this was the first, overwhelming impression – of something walking after it had been put to death. And it walked, really, like someone who might be sleep-walking or like those figures in slow motion one sometimes sees on the screen. It carried a glass, it walked on its toes, the flat hips moved with a dead, horrifying lasciviousness. It seemed to make no sound; this was due to the roar of the bar, which was like the roaring of the sea, heard at night, from far away. It glittered in the dim light; the thin, black hair was violent with oil, combed forward, hanging in bangs; the eyelids gleamed with mascara, the mouth raged with lipstick. The face was white and thoroughly bloodless with some kind of foundation cream; it stank of powder and a gardenia-like perfume. The shirt, open coquettishly to the navel, revealed a hairless chest and a silver crucifix; the shirt was covered with round, paper-thin wafers, red and green and orange and yellow and blue, which stormed in the light and made one feel that the mummy might, at any moment, disappear in flame. A red sash was around the waist, the clinging pants were a surprisingly sombre grey. He wore buckles on his shoes.

I was not sure that he was coming toward me but I could not take my eyes away. He stopped before me, one hand on his hip, looked me up and down, and smiled. He had been eating garlic and his teeth were very bad. His hands, I noticed, with an unbelieving shock, were very large and strong.

'*Eh bien*,' he said, '*il te plait?*'

'*Comment?*' I said.

I really was not sure I had heard him right, though the bright, bright eyes, looking, it seemed, at something amusing within the recess of my skull, did not leave much room for doubt.

'You like him – the barman?'

I did not know what to do or say. It seemed impossible to hit him, it seemed impossible to get angry. It did not seem real, he did not seem real. Besides – no matter what I said, those eyes would mock me with it. I said, as drily as I could:

'How does that concern you?'

'But it concerns me not at all, darling. *Je m'en fou.*'

'Then please get the hell away from me.'

He did not move at once, but smiled at me again. '*Il est dangereux, tu sais.* And for a boy like you – he is *very* dangerous.'

I looked at him. I almost asked him what he meant. 'Go to hell,' I said, and turned my back.

'Oh, no,' he said – and I looked at him again. He was laughing, showing all his teeth – there were not many. 'Oh, no,' he said, 'I go not to hell,' and he clutched his crucifix with one large hand. 'But you, my dear friend – I fear that you shall burn in a very hot fire.' He laughed again. 'Oh, such fire!' He touched his head. 'Here.' And he writhed, as though in torment. 'Every*where*.' And he touched his heart. 'And here.' And he looked at me with malice and mockery and something else; he looked at me as though I was very far away. 'Oh, my poor friend, so young, so strong, so handsome – will you not buy me a drink?'

'*Va te faire foutre.*'

His face crumpled in the sorrow of infants and of very old men

– the sorrow, also, of certain, aging actresses who were renowned in their youth for their fragile, child-like beauty. The dark eyes narrowed in spite and fury and the scarlet mouth turned down like the mask of tragedy. '*Taura du chagrin*,' he said. 'You will be very unhappy. Remember that I told you so.'

And he straightened, as though he were a princess and moved, flaming, away through the crowd.

Then Jacques spoke, at my elbow. 'Everyone in the bar,' he said, 'is talking about how beautifully you and the barman have hit it off.' He gave me a radiant and vindictive smile. 'I trust there has been no confusion?'

I looked down at him. I wanted to do something to his cheerful, hideous, worldly face which would make it impossible for him ever again to smile at anyone the way he was smiling at me. Then I wanted to get out of this bar, out into the air, perhaps to find Hella, my suddenly so sorely menaced girl.

'There's been no confusion,' I snapped. 'Don't you go getting confused, either.'

'I think I can safely say,' said Jacques, 'that I have scarcely ever been less confused than I am at this moment.' He had stopped smiling; he gave me a look which was dry, bitter, and impersonal. 'And, at the risk of losing forever your so remarkably candid friendship, let me tell you something. Confusion is a luxury which only the very, very young can possibly afford, and you are not that young any more.'

'I don't know what you're talking about,' I said. 'Let's have another drink.'

I felt that I had better get drunk. Now Giovanni went behind the bar again and winked at me. Jacques' eyes never left my face. I turned rudely from him and faced the bar again. He followed me.

'The same,' said Jacques.

'Certainly,' said Giovanni, 'that's the way to do it.' He fixed our drinks. Jacques paid. I suppose I did not look too well, for Giovanni shouted at me playfully, 'Eh? Are you drunk already?'

I looked up and smiled. 'You know how Americans drink,' I said. 'I haven't even started yet.'

'David is far from drunk,' said Jacques. 'He is only reflecting bitterly that he must get a new pair of suspenders.'

I could have killed Jacques. Yet it was only with difficulty that I kept myself from laughing. I made a face to signify to Giovanni that the old man was making a private joke, and he disappeared again. That time of evening had come when great batches of people were leaving and great batches were coming in. They would all encounter each other later anyway, in the last bar, all those, that is, unlucky enough to be searching still at such an advanced hour.

I could not look at Jacques; which he knew. He stood beside me, smiling at nothing, humming a tune. There was nothing I could say. I did not dare to mention Hella. I could not even pretend to myself that I was sorry she was in Spain. I was glad. I was utterly, hopelessly, horribly glad. I knew I could do nothing whatever to stop the ferocious excitement which had burst in me like a storm. I could only drink, in the faint hope that the storm might thus spend itself without doing any more damage to my land. But I was glad. I was only sorry that Jacques had been a witness. He made me ashamed. I hated him because he had now seen all that he had waited, often scarcely hoping, so many months to see. We had, in effect, been playing a deadly game and he was the winner. He was the winner in spite of the fact that I had cheated to win.

I wished, nevertheless, standing there at the bar, that I had been able to find in myself the force to turn and walk out – to have gone over to Montparnasse perhaps and picked up a girl. Any girl. I could not do it. I told myself all sorts of lies, standing there at the bar, but I could not move. And this was partly because I knew that it did not really matter any more; it did not even matter if I never spoke to Giovanni again; for they had become visible, as visible as the wafers on the shirt of the flaming princess, they stormed all over me, my awakening, my insistent possibilities.

That was how I met Giovanni. I think we connected the instant that we met. And remain connected still, in spite of our later *separation de corps*, despite the fact that Giovanni will be rotting soon in unhallowed ground near Paris. Until I die there will be those moments, moments seeming to rise up out of the ground like

Macbeth's witches, when his face will come before me, that face in all its changes, when the exact timbre of his voice and tricks of his speech will nearly burst my ears, when his smell will overpower my nostrils. Sometimes, in the days which are coming – God grant me the grace to live them: in the glare of the grey morning, sour-mouthed, eyelids raw and red, hair tangled and damp from my stormy sleep, facing, over coffee and cigarette smoke, last night's impenetrable, meaningless boy who will shortly rise and vanish like the smoke, I will see Giovanni again, as he was that night, so vivid, so winning, all of the light of that gloomy tunnel trapped around his head.

3

At five o'clock in the morning Guillaume locked the door of the bar behind us. The streets were empty and grey. On a corner near the bar a butcher had already opened his shop and one could see him within, already bloody, hacking at the meat. One of the great, green Paris buses lumbered past, nearly empty, its bright electric flag waving fiercely to indicate a turn. A *garçon de café* spilled water on the sidewalk before his establishment and swept it into the gutter. At the end of the long, curving street which faced us were the trees of the boulevard and straw chairs piled high before cafes and the great stone spire of St. Germain des Pres – the most magnificent spire, as Hella and I believed, in Paris. The street beyond the *place* stretched before us to the river and, hidden beside and behind us, meandered to Montparnasse. It was named for an adventurer who sowed a crop in Europe which is being harvested until today. I had often walked this street, sometimes, with Hella, toward the river, often, without her, toward the girls of Montparnasse. Not very long ago either, though it seemed, that morning, to have occurred in another life.

We were going to Les Halles for breakfast. We piled into a taxi, the four of us, unpleasantly crowded together, a circumstance which elicited from Jacques and Guillaume a series of lewd speculations. This lewdness was particularly revolting in that it not only failed of wit, it was so clearly an expression of contempt and self-contempt; it bubbled upward out of them like a fountain of black water. It was clear that they were tantalizing themselves with Giovanni and me and this set my teeth on edge. But Giovanni leaned back against the taxi window, allowing his arm to press my shoulder lightly, seeming to say that we should soon be rid of these old men and should not be distressed that their dirty water splashed – we would have no trouble washing it away.

'Look,' said Giovanni, as we crossed the river. 'This old whore, Paris, as she turns in bed, is very moving.'

I looked out, beyond his heavy profile, which was grey – from fatigue and from the light of the sky above us. The river was swollen and yellow. Nothing moved on the river. Barges were tied up along the banks. The island of the city widened away from us, bearing the weight of the cathedral; beyond this, dimly, through speed and mist, one made out the individual roofs of Paris, their myriad, squat chimney stacks very beautiful and vari-colored under the pearly sky. Mist clung to the river, softening that army of trees, softening those stones, hiding the city's dreadful corkscrew alleys and dead-end streets, clinging like a curse to the men who slept beneath the bridges – one of whom flashed by beneath us, very black and lone, walking along the river.

'Some rats have gone in,' said Giovanni, 'and now other rats come out.' He smiled bleakly and looked at me; to my surprise, he took my hand and held it. 'Have you ever slept under a bridge?' he asked. 'Or perhaps they have soft beds with warm blankets under the bridges in your country?'

I did not know what to do about my hand; it seemed better to do nothing. 'Not yet,' I said, 'but I may. My hotel wants to throw me out.'

I had said it lightly, with a smile, out of a desire to put myself, in terms of an acquaintance with wintry things, on an equal footing with him. But the fact that I had said it as he held my hand made it sound to me unutterably helpless and soft and coy. But I could not say anything to counteract this impression: to say anything more would confirm it. I pulled my hand away, pretending that I had done so in order to search for a cigarette.

Jacques lit it for me.

'Where do you live?' he asked Giovanni.

'Oh,' said Giovanni, 'out. Far out. It is almost not Paris.'

'He lives in a dreadful street, near *Nation*,' said Guillaume, 'among all the dreadful bourgeoisie and their piglike children.'

'You failed to catch the children at the right age,' said Jacques. 'They go through a period, all too brief, *helas!* when a pig is perhaps

the *only* animal they do not call to mind.' And, again to Giovanni:
'In a hotel?'

'No,' said Giovanni, and for the first time he seemed slightly
uncomfortable. 'I live in a maid's room.'

'With the maid?'

'No,' said Giovanni, and smiled, 'the maid is I don't know where.
You could certainly tell that there was no maid if you ever saw my
room.'

'I would love to,' said Jacques.

'Then we will give a party for you one day,' said Giovanni.

This, too courteous and too bald to permit any further question-
ing, nearly forced, nevertheless, a question from my lips. Guillaume
looked briefly at Giovanni, who did not look at him but out into
the morning, whistling. I had been making resolutions for the last
six hours and now I made another one: to have this whole thing
'out' with Giovanni as soon as I got him alone at Les Halles. I was
going to have to tell him that he had made a mistake but that we
could still be friends. But I could not be certain, really, that it might
not be I who was making a mistake, blindly misreading everything
– and out of necessities, then, too shameful to be uttered. I was in
a box for I could see that, no matter how I turned, the hour of
confession was upon me and could scarcely be averted; unless of
course, I leaped out of the cab, which would be the most terrible
confession of all.

Now the cab-driver asked us where we wanted to go, for we had
arrived at the choked boulevards and impassable side-streets of
Les Halles. Leeks, onions, cabbages, oranges, apples, potatoes,
cauliflowers, stood gleaming in mounds all over, on the sidewalks,
in the streets, before great metal sheds. The sheds were blocks long
and within the sheds were piled more fruit, more vegetables, in
some sheds, fish, in some sheds, cheese, in some whole animals,
lately slaughtered. It scarcely seemed possible that all this could
ever be eaten. But in a few hours it would all be gone and trucks
would be arriving from all corners of France – and making their
way, to the great profit of a beehive of middlemen, across the city
of Paris – to feed the roaring multitude. Who were roaring now,

at once wounding and charming the ear, before and behind, and on either side of our taxi – our taxi driver, and Giovanni, too, roared back. The multitude of Paris seems to be dressed in blue everyday but Sunday, when, for the most part, they put on an unbelievably festive black. Here they were now, in blue, disputing, every inch, our passage, with their wagons, handtrucks, camions, their bursting baskets carried at an angle steeply self-confident, on the back. A red-faced woman, burdened with fruit, shouted – to Giovanni, the driver, to the world – a particularly vivid *cochonnerie*, to which the driver and Giovanni, at once, at the top of their lungs, responded, though the fruit lady had already passed beyond our sight and perhaps no longer even remembered her precisely obscene conjectures. We crawled along, for no one had yet told the driver where to stop, and Giovanni and the driver, who had, it appeared, immediately upon entering Les Halles, been transformed into brothers, exchanged speculations, unflattering in the extreme, concerning the hygiene, language, private parts, and habits, of the citizens of Paris. (Jacques and Guillaume were exchanging speculations, unspeakably less good-natured, concerning every passing male.) The pavements were slick with leavings, mainly cast-off, rotten leaves, flowers, fruit and vegetables which had met with disaster natural and slow, or abrupt. And the walls and corners were combed with *pissoirs*, dull-burning, makeshift braziers, cafes, restaurants, and smoky yellow bistros – of these last, some so small that they were little more than diamond shaped, enclosed corners holding bottles and a zinc-covered counter. At all these points, men, young, old, middle-aged, powerful, powerful even in the various fashions in which they had met, or were meeting, their various ruin; and women, more than making up, in shrewdness and patience, in an ability to count and weigh – and shout – whatever they might lack in muscle; though they did not, really, seem to lack much. Nothing here reminded me of home, though Giovanni recognized, revelled in it all.

'I know a place,' he told the driver, '*tres bon marche*' – and told the driver where it was. It developed that it was one of the driver's favorite rendezvous.

'Where is this place?' asked Jacques, petulantly. 'I thought we were going to' – and he named another place.

'You are joking,' said Giovanni, with contempt. 'That place is *very* bad and *very* expensive, it is only for tourists. We are not tourists,' and he added, to me, 'When I first came to Paris I worked in Les Halles – a long time, too, *Nom de Dieu, quelle boulot!* I pray always never to do that again.' And he regarded the streets through which we passed with a sadness which was not less real for being a little theatrical and self-mocking.

Guillaume said, from his corner of the cab: 'Tell him who rescued you.'

'Ah, yes,' said Giovanni, 'behold my saviour, my *patron*.' He was silent a moment. Then: 'You do not regret it, do you? I have not done you any harm? You are pleased with my work?'

'*Mais oui*,' said Guillaume.

Giovanni sighed. '*Bien sûr*.' He looked out of the window again, again whistling. We came to a corner remarkably clear. The taxi stopped.

'*Ici*,' said the driver.

'*Ici*,' Giovanni echoed.

I reached for my wallet but Giovanni sharply caught my hand, conveying to me with an angry flick of his eyelash the intelligence that the least these dirty old men could do was *pay*. He opened the door and stepped out into the street. Guillaume had not reached for his wallet and Jacques paid for the cab.

'Ugh,' said Guillaume, staring at the door of the cafe before which we stood, 'I am sure this place is infested with vermin. Do you want to poison us?'

'It's not the outside you're going to eat,' said Giovanni. 'You are in much more danger of being poisoned in those dreadful, chic places you always go to, where they always have the face clean, *mais, mon Dieu, les fesses!*' He grinned. '*Fais-moi confiance.* Why would I want to poison you? Then I would have no job and I have only just found out that I want to live.'

He and Guillaume, Giovanni still smiling, exchanged a look which I would not have been able to read even if I had dared try;

and Jacques, pushing all of us before him as though we were his chickens, said with that grin: 'We can't stand here in the cold and argue. If we can't eat inside, we can drink. Alcohol kills all microbes.'

And Guillaume brightened suddenly – he was really remarkable, as though he carried, hidden somewhere on his person, a needle filled with vitamins, which automatically, at the blackening hour, discharged itself into his veins. *'Il y a les jeunes dedans,'* he said, and we went in.

Indeed there were young people, half a dozen at the zinc counter before glasses of red and white wine, along with others, not young at all. A pockmarked boy and a very rough-looking girl were playing the pinball machine near the window. There were a few people sitting at the tables in the back, served by an astonishingly clean-looking waiter. In the gloom, the dirty walls, the sawdust-covered floor, his white jacket gleamed like snow. Behind these tables one caught a glimpse of the kitchen and the surly, obese cook. He lumbered about like one of those over-loaded trucks outside, wearing one of those high, white hats, and with a dead cigar stuck between his lips.

Behind the counter sat one of those absolutely inimitable and indomitable ladies, produced only in the city of Paris, but produced there in great numbers, who would be as outraged and unsettling in any other city as a mermaid on a mountain-top. All over Paris they sit behind their counters like a mother bird in a nest and brood over the cash-register as though it were an egg. Nothing occurring under the circle of heaven where they sit escapes their eye, if they have ever been surprised by anything, it was only in a dream – a dream they long ago ceased having. They are neither ill- nor good-natured, though they have their days and styles, and they know, in the way, apparently, that other people know when they have to go to the bathroom, everything about everyone who enters their domain. Though some are white-haired and some not, some fat, some thin, some grandmothers and some but lately virgins, they all have exactly the same shrewd, vacant, all-registering eye; it is difficult to believe that they ever cried for milk, or looked at the sun; it seems they must have come into the world hungry for banknotes, and squinting helplessly, unable to focus their eyes until they came to rest on a cash-register.

This one's hair is black and grey and she has a face which comes from Brittany; and she, like almost everyone else standing at the bar, knows Giovanni and, after her fashion, likes him. She has a big, deep bosom and she clasps Giovanni to it; and a big, deep voice.

'*Ah, mon pote!*' she cries. '*Tu es revenu!* You have come back at last! *Salaud!* Now that you are rich and have found rich friends you never come to see us any more! *Canaille!*'

And she beams at us, the 'rich' friends, with a friendliness deliciously, deliberately vague; she would have no trouble reconstructing every instant of our biographies from the moment we were born until this morning. She knows exactly who is rich – and how rich – and she knows it isn't me. For this reason, perhaps, there was a click of speculation infinitesimally double behind her eyes when she looked at me. In a moment, however, she knows that she will understand it all.

'You know how it is,' says Giovanni, extricating himself and throwing back his hair, 'when you work, when you become serious, you have no time to play.'

'*Tiens,*' she says, with mockery. '*Sans blague?*'

'But I assure you,' says Giovanni, 'even when you are a young man like me, you get very tired' – she laughs – 'and you go to sleep early' – she laughs again – 'and *alone,*' says Giovanni, as though this proved everything, and she clicks her teeth in sympathy and laughs again.

'And now,' she says, 'are you coming or going? Have you come for breakfast or have you come for a nightcap? *Nom de Dieu,* you do not *look* very serious, I believe you need a drink.'

'*Bien sûr,*' says someone at the bar, 'after such hard work he needs a bottle of white wine – and perhaps a few dozen oysters.'

Everybody laughs. Everybody, without seeming to, is looking at us and I am beginning to feel like part of a travelling circus. Everybody, also, seems very proud of Giovanni.

Giovanni turns to the voice at the bar. 'An excellent idea, friend,' he says, 'and exactly what I had in mind.' Now he turns to us. 'You have not met my friends,' he says, looking at me, then at the woman. 'This is Monsieur Guillaume,' he tells her, and with the most subtle flattening of his voice, 'my *patron*. He can tell you if I am serious.'

'Ah,' she dares to say, 'but I cannot tell if *he* is,' and covers this daring with a laugh.

Guillaume, raising his eyes with difficulty from the young men at the bar, stretches out his hand and smiles. 'But you are right, Madame,' he says. 'He is so much more serious than I am that I fear he will own my bar one day.'

He will when lions fly, she is thinking, but professes herself enchanted by him and shakes his hand with energy.

'And Monsieur Jacques,' says Giovanni, 'one of our finest customers.'

'*Enchanté, Madame,*' says Jacques, with his most dazzling smile, of which she, in responding, produces the most artless parody.

'And this is *monsieur l'americain,*' says Giovanni, 'otherwise known as: *Monsieur David. Madame Clothilde.*'

And he stands back slightly. Something is burning in his eyes and it lights up all his face, it is joy and pride.

'*Je suis ravi, monsieur,*' she tells me and looks at me and shakes my hand and smiles.

I am smiling too, I scarcely know why; everything in me is jumping up and down. Giovanni carelessly puts an arm round my shoulder. 'What have you got good to eat?' he cried. 'We are hungry.'

'But we must have a drink first!' cried Jacques.

'But we can drink sitting down,' said Giovanni, 'no?'

'No,' said Guillaume, to whom leaving the bar, at the moment, would have seemed like being driven from the promised land, 'let us first have a drink, here at the bar, with Madame.'

Guillaume's suggestion had the effect – but subtly, as though a wind had blown over everything or a light been imperceptibly intensified – of creating among the people at the bar, a *troupe*, who would now play various roles in a play they knew very well. Madame Clothilde would demur, as, indeed, she instantly did, but only for a moment; then she would accept, it would be something expensive; it turned out to be champagne. She would sip it, making the most noncommittal conversation, so that she could vanish out of it a split-second before Guillaume had established contact with one of the boys at the bar. As for the boys at the bar, they were each invisibly preening, having already calculated how much money he and his *copain* would need for the next few days, having already appraised Guillaume to within a decimal of that figure, and having already estimated how long Guillaume, as a fountainhead, would last, and also how long they would be able to endure him. The only question left was whether they would be *vache* with him, or *chic*, but they knew that they would probably be *vache*. There was also Jacques, who might turn out to be a bonus, or merely a consolation prize. There was me, of course, another matter altogether, innocent of apartments, soft beds, or food, a candidate, therefore, for affection, but, as Giovanni's *mome*, out of honorable reach. Their only means, practically at least, of conveying their affection for Giovanni and me was to relieve us of these two old men. So that there was added, to the roles they were about to play, a certain, jolly aura of conviction and, to self-interest, an altruistic glow.

I ordered black coffee and a cognac, a large one. Giovanni was far from me, drinking *marc* between an old man who looked like a receptacle of all the world's dirt and disease and a young boy, a redhead, who would look like that man one day, if one could read, in the dullness of his eye, anything so real as a future. Now, however, he had something of a horse's dreadful beauty; some suggestion, too, of the storm trooper; covertly, he was watching Guillaume; he knew that both Guillaume and Jacques were watching him. Guillaume chatted, meanwhile, with Madame Clothilde, they were agreeing that business was awful, that all standards had been debased by the *nouveau riche*, and that the country needed de Gaulle. Luckily they had both had this conversation so many times before that it ran, so to speak, all by itself, demanding of them nothing in the way of concentration. Jacques would, shortly, offer one of the boys a drink but, for the moment, he wished to play uncle to me.

'How do you feel?' he asked me. 'This is a very important day for you.'

'I feel fine,' I said. 'How do you feel?'

'Like a man,' he said, 'who has seen a vision.'

'Yes?' I said. 'Tell me about this vision.'

'I am not joking,' he said. 'I am talking about you. *You* were the vision. You should have seen yourself tonight. You should see yourself now.'

I looked at him and said nothing.

'You are – how old? Twenty-six or -seven? I am nearly twice that and, let me tell you, you are lucky. You are lucky that what is happening to you now is happening *now* and not when you are forty, or something like that, when there would be no hope for you and you would simply be destroyed.'

'What is happening to me?' I asked. I had meant to sound sardonic but I did not sound sardonic at all.

He did not answer this, but sighed, looking briefly in the direction of the redhead. Then he turned to me. 'Are you going to write to Hella?'

'I very often do,' I said. 'I suppose I will again.'

'That does not answer my question.'

'Oh. I was under the impression that you had asked me if I was going to write to Hella.'

'Well. Let's put it another way. Are you going to write to Hella about this night and this morning?'

'I really don't see what there is to write about. But what's it to you if I do or I don't?'

He gave me a look full of a certain despair which I had not till that moment, known was in him. It frightened me. 'It's not,' he said, 'what it is to *me*. It's what it is to *you*. And to her. And to that poor boy, yonder, who doesn't know that when he looks at you the way he does, he is simply putting his head in the lion's mouth. Are you going to treat him as you've treated me?'

'*You?* What have *you* to do with all this? How have I treated *you?*'

'You have been very unfair to me,' he said. 'You have been very dishonest.'

This time I did sound sardonic. 'I suppose you mean that I would have been fair, I would have been honest if I had – if –'

'I mean you could have been fair to me by despising me a little less.'

'I'm sorry. But I think, since you bring it up, that a lot of your life *is* despicable.'

'I could say the same about yours,' said Jacques. 'There are so many ways of being despicable it quite makes one's head spin. But the way to be really despicable is to be contemptuous of other people's pain. You ought to have some apprehension that the man you see before you was once even younger than you are now and arrived at his present wretchedness by imperceptible degrees.'

There was silence for a moment, threatened, from a distance, by that laugh of Giovanni's.

'Tell me,' I said at last, 'is there really no other way for you but this? To kneel down forever before an army of boys for just five dirty minutes in the dark?'

'Think,' said Jacques, 'of the men who have kneeled before you while you thought of something else and pretended that nothing was happening down there in the dark between your legs.'

I stared at the amber cognac and at the wet rings on the metal. Deep below, trapped in the metal, the outline of my own face looked upward hopelessly at me.

'You think,' he persisted, 'that my life is shameful because my encounters are. And they are. But you should ask yourself *why* they are.'

'Why are they – shameful?' I asked him.

'Because there is no affection in them, and no joy. It's like putting an electric plug in a dead socket. Touch, but no contact. All touch, but no contact and no light.'

I asked him: 'Why?'

'That you must ask yourself,' he told me, 'and perhaps one day this morning will not be ashes in your mouth.'

I looked over at Giovanni, who now had one arm around the

49

ruined-looking girl, who could have once been very beautiful but who never would be now.

Jacques followed my look. 'He is very fond of you,' he said, 'already. But this doesn't make you happy or proud, as it should. It makes you frightened and ashamed. Why?'

'I don't understand him,' I said at last. 'I don't know what his friendship means, I don't know what he means by friendship.'

Jacques laughed. 'You don't know what he means by friendship but you have the feeling it may not be safe. You are afraid it may change you. What kind of friendship have you had?'

I said nothing.

'Or for that matter,' he continued, 'what kind of love affairs?'

I was silent for so long that he teased me, saying, 'Come out, come out, wherever you are!'

And I grinned, feeling chilled.

'Love him,' said Jacques, with vehemence, 'love him and let him love you. Do you think anything else under heaven really matters? And how long, at the best, can it last, since you are both men and still have everywhere to go? Only five minutes, I assure you, only five minutes, and most of that, *helas*! in the dark. And if you think of them as dirty, then they *will* be dirty – they will be dirty because you will be giving nothing, you will be despising your flesh and his. But you can make your time together anything but dirty, you can give each other something which will make both of you better – forever – if you will *not* be ashamed, if you will only *not* play it safe.' He paused, watching me, and then looked down to his cognac. 'You play it safe long enough,' he said, in a different tone, 'and you'll end up trapped in your own dirty body, forever and' forever and forever – like me.' And he finished his cognac, ringing his glass slightly on the bar to attract the attention of Madame Clothilde.

She came at once, beaming; and in that moment Guillaume dared to smile at the redhead. Mme. Clothilde poured Jacques a fresh cognac and looked questioningly at me, the bottle poised over my half full glass. I hesitated.

'*Et pourquoi pas?*' she asked, with a smile.

So I finished my glass and she filled it. Then, for the briefest of seconds, she glanced at Guillaume; who cried, '*Et le rouquin là!* what's the redhead drinking?'

Mme. Clothilde turned with the air of an actress about to deliver the severely restrained last lines of an exhausting and mighty part. '*On t'offre, Pierre*,' she said, majestically. 'What will you have?' – holding slightly aloft meanwhile the bottle containing the most expensive cognac in the house.

'*Je prendrai un petit cognac*,' Pierre mumbled after a moment and, oddly enough, he blushed, which made him, in the light of the pale, just rising sun, resemble a freshly fallen angel.

Mme. Clothilde filled Pierre's glass and, amid a beautifully resolving tension, as of slowly dimming lights, replaced the bottle on the shelf and walked back to the cash-register; offstage, in effect, into the wings, where she began to recover herself by finishing the last of the champagne. She sighed and sipped and looked outward contentedly into the slowly rising morning. Guillaume had murmured a '*Je m'excuse un instant, Madame*,' and now passed behind us on his way to the redhead.

I smiled. 'Things my father never told me.'

'*Somebody*,' said Jacques, 'your father or mine, should have told us that not many people have ever died of love. But multitudes have perished, and are perishing every hour – and in the oddest places! – for the lack of it.' And then: 'Here comes your baby. *Sois sage. Sois chic*.'

He moved slightly away and began talking to the boy next to him.

And here my baby came indeed, through all that sunlight, his face flushed and his hair flying, his eyes, unbelievably, like morning stars. 'It was not very nice of me to go off for so long,' he said, 'I hope you have not been too bored.'

'*You* certainly haven't been,' I said to him. 'You look like a kid about five years old waking up on Christmas morning.'

This delighted, even flattered him, as I could see from the way he now humorously pursed his lips. 'I am sure I cannot look like that,' he said. 'I was always disappointed on Christmas morning.'

'Well, I mean very *early* on Christmas morning, before you saw what was under the tree.' But his eyes have somehow made of my last statement a *double entendre*, and we are both laughing.

'Are you hungry?' he asked.

'Perhaps I would be if I were alive and sober. I don't know. Are you?'

'I think we should eat,' he said, with no conviction whatever, and we began to laugh again.

'Well,' I said, 'what shall we eat?'

'I scarcely dare suggest white wine and oysters,' said Giovanni, 'but that is really the best thing after such a night.'

'Well, let's do that,' I said, 'while we can still walk to the dining room.' I looked beyond him to Guillaume and the redhead, they had apparently found something to talk about, I could not imagine what it was; and Jacques was deep in conversation with the tall, very young, pockmarked boy, whose turtleneck black sweater made him seem even paler and thinner than he actually was. He had been playing the pinball machine when we came in, his name appeared to be Yves. 'Are they going to eat now?' I asked Giovanni.

'Perhaps not now,' said Giovanni, 'but they are certainly going to eat. Everyone is very hungry.' I took this to refer more to the boys than to our friends, and we passed into the dining room, which was now empty, the waiter nowhere in sight.

'Mme. Clothilde!' shouted Giovanni, *'on mange ici, non?'*

This shout produced an answering shout from Mme. Clothilde and also produced the waiter, whose jacket was less spotless, seen in closeup, than it had seemed from a distance. It also officially announced our presence in the dining room to Jacques and Guillaume and must have definitely increased, in the eyes of the boys they were talking to, a certain tigerish intensity of affection.

'We'll eat quickly and go,' said Giovanni. 'After all, I have to work tonight.'

'Did you meet Guillaume here?' I asked him.

He grimaced, looking down. 'No. That is a long story.' He grinned. 'No, I did not meet him here. I met him' – he laughed – 'in a cinema!' We both laughed. *'C'etait un film du far west, avec*

Gary Cooper.' This seemed terribly funny, too, we kept laughing until the waiter came with our bottle of white wine.

'Well,' said Giovanni, sipping the wine, his eyes damp, 'after the last gun-shot had been fired and all the music came up to celebrate the triumph of goodness and I came up the aisle, I bumped into this man – Guillaume – and I excused myself and walked into the lobby. Then here he came, after me, with a long story about leaving his scarf in *my* seat because, it appeared, he had been sitting *behind* me, you understand, with his coat and his scarf on the seat *before* him and when I sat down I pulled his scarf down with me. Well, I told him I didn't work for the cinema and I told him what he could do with his scarf – but I did not really get angry because he made me want to laugh. He said that all the people who worked for the cinema were thieves and he was sure that they would keep it if they so much as laid eyes on it, and it was very expensive, and a gift from his mother and – oh, I assure you, not even Garbo ever gave such a performance. So I went back and of course there was no scarf there and when I told him this it seemed he would fall dead right there in the lobby. And by this time, you understand, everybody thought we were together and I didn't know whether to kick him or the people who were looking at us; but he was very well dressed, of course, and I was not and so I thought, well, we had better get out of this lobby. So we went to a cafe and sat on the terrace and when he had got over his grief about the scarf and what his mother would say and so on and so on, he asked me to have supper with him. Well, naturally, I said no, I had certainly had enough of him by that time, but the only way I could prevent another scene, right there on the terrace, was to promise to have supper with him a few days later – I did not intend to go,' he said, with a shy grin, 'but when the day came I had not eaten for a long time and I was very hungry.' He looked at me and I saw in his face again something which I have fleetingly seen there during these hours: under his beauty and his bravado, terror, and a terrible desire to please; dreadfully moving, and it made me want, in anguish, to reach out and comfort him.

Our oysters came and we began to eat. Giovanni sat in the sun, his black hair gathering to itself the yellow glow of the wine and the many dull colors of the oyster where the sun struck it.

'Well' – with his mouth turned down – 'dinner was awful, of course, since he can make scenes in his apartment, too. But by this time I knew he owned a bar and was a French citizen. I am not and I had no job and no *carte de travail*. So I saw that he could be useful if I could only find some way to make him keep his hands off me. I did not, I must say' – this with that look at me – 'altogether succeed in remaining untouched by him, he has more hands than an octopus, and no dignity whatever, *but*' – grimly throwing down another oyster and refilling our glasses of wine – 'I *do* now have a *carte de travail* and I have a job. Which pays very well,' he grinned, 'it appears that I am good for business. For this reason, he leaves me mostly alone.' He looked out into the bar. 'He is really not a man at all,' he said, with a sorrow and bewilderment at once childlike and ancient, 'I do not know what he is, he is horrible. But I will keep my *carte de travail*. The job is another matter, but' – he knocked wood – 'we have had no trouble now for nearly three weeks.'

'But you think that trouble is coming,' I said.

'Oh, yes,' said Giovanni, with a quick, startled look at me, as if he were wondering if I had understood a word of what he had said, 'we are certainly going to have a little trouble soon again. Not right away, of course, that is not his style. But he will invent something to be angry at me about.'

Then we sat in silence for a while, smoking cigarettes, surrounded by oyster shells, and finishing the wine. I was all at once very tired. I looked out into the narrow street, this strange, crooked corner where we sat, which was brazen now with the sunlight and heavy with people – people I would never understand. I ached abruptly, intolerably, with a longing to go home; not to that hotel, in one of the alleys of Paris, where the concierge barred the way with my unpaid bill; but home, home across the ocean, to things and people I knew and understood; to those things, those places, those people which I would always helplessly, and in whatever bitterness of spirit, love above all else. I had never realized such a sentiment in myself before, and it frightened me. I saw myself, sharply, as a wanderer, an adventurer, rocking through the world, unanchored. I looked at Giovanni's face, which did not help me. He belonged to this strange city, which did not belong to me. I began to see that, while what was happening to me was not so strange as it would have comforted me to believe, yet it was strange beyond belief. It was not really so strange, so unprecedented, though voices deep within me boomed, For shame! For shame! that I should be so abruptly, so hideously entangled with a boy; what was strange was that this was but one tiny aspect of the dreadful human tangle, occurring everywhere, without end, forever.

'*Viens*,' said Giovanni.

We rose and walked back into the bar and Giovanni paid our bill. Another bottle of champagne had been opened and Jacques and Guillaume were now really beginning to be drunk. It was going to be ghastly and I wondered if those poor, patient boys were ever going to get anything to eat. Giovanni talked to Guillaume for a moment, agreeing to open up the bar; Jacques was too busy with the pale, tall boy to have much time for me; we said good-morning and left them.

'I must go home,' I said to Giovanni when we were in the street. 'I must pay my hotel bill.'

Giovanni stared. '*Mais tu es fou*,' he said, mildly. 'There is certainly no point in going home now, to face an ugly concierge and then go to sleep in that room all by yourself and then wake up later, with a terrible stomach and a sour mouth, wanting to commit suicide. Come with me, we will rise at a civilized hour, and have a gentle aperitif somewhere and then a little dinner. It will be much more cheerful like that,' he said, with a smile, 'you will see.'

'But I must get my clothes,' I said.

He took my arm. '*Bien sûr*. But you do not have to get them *now*.' I held back. He stopped. 'Come. I am sure that I am much prettier than your wallpaper – or your concierge. I will smile at you when you wake up. They will not.'

'Ah,' I could only say, '*tu es vache*.'

'It is you who are *vache*,' he said, 'to want to leave me alone in this lonely place when you know that I am far too drunk to reach my home unaided.'

We laughed together, both caught up in a stinging, teasing sort of game. We reached the Boulevard Sebastopol. 'But we will not any longer discuss the painful subject of how you desired to desert Giovanni, at so dangerous an hour, in the middle of a hostile city.' I began to realize that he, too, was nervous. Far down the boulevard a cab meandered toward us, and he put up his hand. 'I will show you my room,' he said, 'it is perfectly clear that you would have to see it one of these days, anyway.' The taxi stopped beside us, and Giovanni, as though he were suddenly afraid that I would really turn and run, pushed me in before him. He got in beside me and told the driver: '*Nation.*'

The street he lived on was wide, respectable rather than elegant, and massive with fairly recent apartment buildings; the street ended in a small park. His room was in the back, on the ground floor of the last building on this street. We passed the vestibule and the elevator into a short, dark corridor which led to his room. The room was small, I only made out the outlines of clutter and disorder, there was the smell of the alcohol he burned in his stove. He locked the door behind us, and then for a moment, in the gloom, we simply stared at each other – with dismay, with relief, and breathing hard. I was trembling. I thought, if I do not open the door at once and get out of here, I am lost. But I knew I could not open the door, I knew it was too late; soon it was too late to do anything but moan. He pulled me against him, putting himself into my arms as though he were giving me himself to carry, and slowly pulled me down with him to that bed. With everything in me screaming *No!* yet the sum of me sighed *Yes.*

Here in the south of France it does not often snow; but snowflakes, in the beginning rather gently and now with more force, have been falling for the last half hour. It falls as though it might quite possibly decide to turn into a blizzard. It has been cold down here this winter, though the people of the region seem to take it as a mark of ill-breeding in a foreigner if he makes any reference to this fact. They themselves, even when their faces are burning in that wind which seems to blow from everywhere at once, and which penetrates everything, are as radiantly cheerful as children at the sea-shore. '*Il fait beau bien?*' – throwing their faces toward the lowering sky in which the celebrated southern sun has not made an appearance in days.

I leave the window of the big room and walk through the house. While I am in the kitchen, staring into the mirror – I have decided to shave before all the water turns cold – I hear a knocking at the door. Some vague, wild hope leaps in me for a second and then I realize that it is only the caretaker from across the road, come to make certain that I have not stolen the silver, or smashed the dishes or chopped up the furniture for firewood. And, indeed, she rattles the door and I hear her voice out there, cracking, '*M'sieu! M'sieu! M'sieu, l'americain!*' I wonder, with annoyance, why on earth she should sound so worried.

But she smiles at once when I open the door, a smile which weds the coquette and the mother. She is quite old and not really French; she came many years ago, 'when I was a very young girl, sir,' from just across the border, out of Italy. She seems, like most of the women down here, to have gone into mourning directly the last child moved out of childhood. Hella thought that they were all widows, but, it turned out, most of them had husbands living yet. These husbands might have been their sons. They sometimes played *Pelote* in the sunshine in a flat field near our house, and their eyes, when they looked at Hella, contained the proud watchfulness of a father and the watchful speculation of a man. I sometimes played billiards with them, and drank red wine, in the *tabac*. But they made me tense – with their ribaldries, their good-nature, their fellowship, the life written on their hands and in their faces and in their eyes. They treated me as the son who has but lately been initiated into manhood; but at the same time, with great distance, for I did not really belong to any of them; and they also sensed (or I felt they did) something else about me, something which it was no longer worth their while to pursue. This seemed to be in their eyes when I walked with Hella and they passed us on the road, saying, very respectfully, *Salut, Monsieur-dame.* They might have been the sons of these women in black, come home after a lifetime of storming and conquering the world, home, to rest and be scolded and wait for death, home to those breasts, now dry, which had nourished them in their beginnings.

Flakes of snow have drifted across the shawl which covers her head; and hang on her eyelashes and on the wisps of black and white hair not covered by the shawl. She is very strong yet, though, now, a little bent, a little breathless.

'*Bonsoir, monsieur. Vous n'etes pas malade?*'

'No,' I say, 'I have not been sick. Come in.'

She comes in, closing the door behind her, and allowing the shawl to fall from her head. I still have my drink in my hand and she notices this, in silence.

'*Eh bien,*' she says. '*Tant mieux.* But we have not seen you for several days. You have been staying in the house?'

And her eyes search my face.

I am embarrassed and resentful; yet it is impossible to rebuff something at once shrewd and gentle in her eyes and voice. 'Yes,' I say, 'the weather has been bad.'

'It is not the middle of August, to be sure,' says she, 'but you do not have the air of an invalid. It is not good to sit in the house alone.'

'I am leaving in the morning,' I say, desperately. 'Did you want to take the inventory?'

'Yes,' she says, and produces from one of her pockets the list of household goods I signed upon arrival. 'It will not be long. Let me start from the back.'

We start toward the kitchen. On the way I put my drink down on the night table in my bedroom.

'It doesn't matter to me if you drink,' she says, not turning around. But I leave my drink behind anyway.

We walk into the kitchen. The kitchen is suspiciously clean and neat. 'Where have you been eating?' she asks sharply. 'They tell me at the *tabac* you have not been seen for days. Have you been going to town?'

'Yes,' I say, lamely, 'sometimes.'

'On foot?' she inquires. 'Because the bus driver, he has not seen you, either.' All this time she is not looking at me but around the kitchen, checking off the list in her hand with a short, yellow pencil.

I can make no answer to her last, sardonic thrust, having forgotten that in a small village almost every move is made under the village's collective eye and ear.

She looks briefly in the bathroom. 'I'm going to clean that tonight,' I say.

'I should hope so,' she says. 'Everything was clean when you moved in.' We walk back through the kitchen. She has failed to notice that two glasses are missing, broken by me, and I have not the energy to tell her. I will leave some money in the cupboard. She turns on the light in the guest-room. My dirty clothes are lying all over.

'Those go with me,' I say, trying to smile.

'You could have come just across the road,' she says. 'I would have been glad to give you something to eat. A little soup, something nourishing. I cook every day for my husband, what difference does one more make?'

This touches me, but I do not know how to indicate it, and I cannot say, of course, that eating with her and her husband would have stretched my nerves to the breaking point.

She is examining a decorative pillow. 'Are you going to join your fiancée?' she asks.

I know I ought to lie, but, somehow, I cannot. I am afraid of her eyes. I wish, now, that I had my drink with me. 'No,' I say, flatly, 'she has gone to America.'

'*Tiens!*' she says. 'And you – do you stay in France?' She looks directly at me.

'For awhile,' I say. I am beginning to sweat. It has come to me that this woman, a peasant from Italy, must resemble, in so many ways, the mother of Giovanni. I keep trying not to hear her howls of anguish, I keep trying not to see in her eyes what would surely be there if she knew that her son would be dead by morning, if she knew what I had done to her son.

59

But of course, she is not Giovanni's mother.

'It is not good,' she says, 'it is not right for a young man like you to be sitting alone in a great big house with no woman.' She looks, for a moment, very sad; starts to say something more and thinks better of it. I know she wants to say something about Hella, whom neither she, nor any of the other women here had liked. But she turns out the light in the guest room and we go into the big bedroom, the master bedroom, which Hella and I had used, not the one in which I have left my drink. This, too, is very clean and orderly. She looks about the room and looks at me, and smiles.

'You have not been using this room lately,' she says.

I feel myself blushing painfully. She laughs.

'But you will be happy again,' she says. 'You must go and find yourself another woman, a *good* woman, and get married, and have babies. *Yes*, that is what you ought to do,' she says, as though I had contradicted her, and before I can say anything, 'Where is your *maman*?'

'She is dead.'

'Ah!' She clicks her teeth in sympathy. 'That is sad. And your Papa – is he dead, too?'

'No. He is in America.'

'*Pauvre bambino!*' She looks at my face. I am really helpless in front of her and if she does not leave soon she will reduce me to tears or curses. 'But you do not have the intention of just wandering through the world like a sailor? I am sure that would make your mother very unhappy. You will make a home someday?'

'Yes, surely. Someday.'

She puts her strong hand on my arm. 'Even if your *maman*, she is dead – that is very sad! – your Papa will be very happy to see bambinos from you.' She pauses, her black eyes soften; she is looking at me, but she is looking beyond me, too. 'We had three sons. Two of them were killed in the war. In the war, too, we lost all our money. It is sad, is it not, to have worked so hard all one's life in order to have a little peace in one's old age and then to have it all taken away? It almost killed my husband, he has never been the same since.' Then I see that her eyes are not merely shrewd, they are also bitter and very sad. She shrugs her shoulders. 'Ah! What can one do? It is better not to think about it.' Then she smiles. 'But our last son, he lived in the north, he came to see us two years ago, and he brought with him his little boy. His little boy, he was only four years old then. He was so beautiful! Mario, he is called.' She gestures. 'It is my husband's name. They stayed about ten days and we felt young again.' She smiles again. 'Especially my husband.' And she stands there a moment with this smile on her face. Then she asks, abruptly, 'Do you pray?'

I wonder if I can stand this another moment. 'No,' I stammer. 'No. Not often.'

'But you are a believer?'

I smile. It is not even a patronizing smile, though, perhaps, I wish it could be. 'Yes.'

But I wonder what my smile could have looked like. It did not reassure her. 'You must pray,' she says, very soberly. 'I assure you. Even just a little prayer, from time to time. Light a little candle. If it were not for the prayers of the blessed saints one could not live in this world at all. I speak to you,' she says, drawing herself up slightly, 'as though I were your *maman*. Do not be offended.'

'But I am not offended. You are very nice. You are very nice to speak to me this way.'

She smiles a satisfied smile. 'Men – not just babies like you, but old men, too – they always need a woman to tell them the truth. *Les hommes, ils sont impossible.*' And she smiles, and forces me to smile at the cunning of this universal joke, and turns out the light in the master bedroom. We go down the hall again, thank heaven, to my drink. This bedroom of course, is quite untidy, the light burning, my bathrobe, books, dirty socks, and a couple of dirty glasses, and a coffee cup half full of stale coffee – lying around, all over the place: and the sheets on the bed a tangled mess.

'I'll fix this up before morning,' I say.

'*Bien sûr.*' She sighs. 'You really must take my advice, monsieur, and get married.' At this, suddenly, we both laugh. Then I finish my drink.

The inventory is almost done. We go into the last big room,

where the bottle is, before the window. She looks at the bottle, then at me. 'But you will be drunk by morning,' she says.

'Oh, no! I'm taking the bottle *with* me.'

It is quite clear that she knows this is not true. But she shrugs her shoulders again. Then she becomes, by the act of wrapping the shawl around her head, very formal, even a little shy. Now that I see she is about to leave I wish I could think of something to make her stay. When she has gone back across the road, the night will be blacker and longer than ever. I have something to say to her – to her? – but of course it will never be said. I feel that I want to be forgiven, I want *her* to forgive me. But I do not know how to state my crime. My crime, in some odd way, is in being a man and she knows all about this already. It is terrible how naked she makes me feel, like a half grown boy, naked before his mother.

She puts out her hand. I take it, awkwardly.

'*Bon voyage, monsieur*, I hope that you were happy while you were here and that, perhaps, one day, you will visit us again' She is smiling and her eyes are kind but now the smile is purely social, it is the graceful termination of a business deal.

'Thank you,' I say. 'Perhaps I will be back next year.' She releases my hand and we walk to the door.

'Oh!' she says, at the door, 'please do not wake me up in the morning. Put the keys in my mailbox. I do not, any more, have any reason to get up so early.'

'Surely.' I smile and open the door. 'Goodnight, Madame.'

'*Bonsoir, Monsieur. Adieu!*' She steps out into the darkness. But there is a light coming from my house and from her house across the road. The town lights glimmer beneath us and I hear, briefly, the sea again.

She walks a little away from me, and turns. '*Souvenez-vous,*' she tells me. 'One must make a little prayer from time to time.'

And I close the door.

She has made me realize that I have much to do before morning. I decide to clean the bathroom before I allow myself another drink. And I begin to do this, first scrubbing out the tub, then running water into the pail to mop the floor. The bathroom is tiny and square, with one frosted window. It reminds me of that claustrophobic room in Paris. Giovanni had had great plans for remodeling the room and there was a time, when he had actually begun to do this, when we lived with plaster all over everything and bricks piled on the floor. We took packages of bricks out of the house at night and left them in the streets.

I suppose they will come for him early in the morning, perhaps just before dawn, so that the last thing Giovanni will ever see will be that grey, lightless sky over Paris, beneath which we stumbled homeward together so many desperate and drunken mornings.

Part Two

I

I remember that life in that room seemed to be occurring beneath the sea, time flowed past indifferently above us, hours and days had no meaning. In the beginning our life together held a joy and amazement which was newborn every day. Beneath the joy, of course, was anguish and beneath the amazement was fear; but they did not work themselves to the beginning until our high beginning was aloes on our tongues. By then anguish and fear had become the surface on which we slipped and slid, losing balance, dignity, and pride. Giovanni's face, which I had memorized so many mornings, noons, and nights, hardened before my eyes, began to give in secret places, began to crack. The light in the eyes became a glitter, the wide and beautiful brow began to suggest the skull beneath. The sensual lips turned inward, busy with the sorrow overflowing from his heart. It became a stranger's face – or it made me so guilty to look on him that I wished it were a stranger's face. Not all my memorizing had prepared me for the metamorphosis which my memorizing had helped to bring about.

Our day began before daybreak, when I drifted over to Guillaume's bar in time for a pre-closing drink. Sometimes, when Guillaume had closed the bar to the public, a few friends and Giovanni and myself stayed behind for breakfast and music. Sometimes Jacques was there – from the time of our meeting with Giovanni he seemed to come out more and more. If we had breakfast with Guillaume, we usually left around seven o'clock in the morning. Sometimes, when Jacques was there, he offered to drive us home in the car which he had suddenly and inexplicably bought, but we almost always walked the long way home along the river.

Spring was approaching Paris. Walking up and down this house tonight, I see again the river, the cobblestoned *quais*, the bridges. Low boats passed beneath the bridges and on those boats one sometimes saw women hanging washing out to dry. Sometimes we saw a young man in a canoe, energetically rowing, looking rather helpless, and, also, rather silly. There were yachts tied up along the banks from time to time, and house-boats, and barges; we passed the firehouse so often on our way home that the firemen got to know us. When winter came again and Giovanni found himself in hiding in one of these barges, it was a fireman, who, seeing him crawl back into hiding with a loaf of bread one night, tipped off the police.

The trees grew green those mornings, the river dropped, and the brown winter smoke dropped downward out of it, and fishermen appeared. Giovanni was right about the fishermen, they certainly never seemed to catch anything, but it gave them something to do. Along the *quais* the bookstalls seemed to become almost festive, awaiting the weather which would allow the passerby to leaf idly through the dog-eared books, and which would inform the tourist with a passionate desire to carry off to the United States, or Denmark, more colored prints than he could afford, or, when he got home, know what to do with. Also, the girls appeared on their bicycles, along with boys similarly equipped, and we sometimes saw them along the river, as the light began to fade, their bicycles put away until the morrow. This was after Giovanni had lost his job and we walked around in the evenings. Those evenings were bitter. Giovanni knew that I was going to leave him but he did not dare accuse me for fear of being corroborated. I did not dare tell him. Hella was on her way back from Spain and my father had agreed to send me money, which I was not going to use to help Giovanni, who had done so much to help me. I was going to use it to escape his room.

Every morning the sky and the sun seemed to be a little higher and the river stretched before us with a greater haze of promise. Every day the book-stall keepers seemed to have taken off another garment, so that the shape of their bodies appeared to be undergoing a most striking and continual metamorphosis. One began to wonder what the final shape would be. It was observable, through open windows on the *quais* and sidestreets, that *hoteliers* had called in painters to paint the rooms; the women in the dairies had taken off their blue sweaters and rolled up the sleeves of their dresses, so that one saw their powerful arms; the bread seemed warmer and fresher in the bakeries. The small school children had taken off their capes and their knees were no longer scarlet with the cold. There seemed to be more chatter – in that curiously measured and vehement language, which sometimes reminds me of stiffening egg white and sometimes of stringed instruments but always of the underside and aftermath of passion.

But we did not often have breakfast in Guillaume's bar because Guillaume did not like me. Usually I simply waited around, as inconspicuously as possible, until Giovanni had finished cleaning up the bar and had changed his clothes. Then we said good-night and left. The habitués had evolved toward us a curious attitude, composed of an unpleasant maternalism, and envy, and disguised dislike. They could not, somehow, speak to us as they spoke to one another and they resented the strain we imposed on them of speaking in any other way. And it made them furious that the dead center of their lives was, in this instance, none of their business. It made them feel their poverty again, through the narcotics of chatter, and dreams of conquest, and mutual contempt.

Wherever we ate breakfast, and wherever we walked, when we got home we were always too tired to sleep right away. We made coffee and sometimes drank cognac with it; we sat on the bed and talked and smoked. We seemed to have a great deal to tell – or Giovanni did. Even at my most candid, even when I tried hardest to give myself to him as he gave himself to me, I was holding something back. I did not, for example, really tell him about Hella until I had been living in the room a month. I told him about her then because her letters had begun to sound as though she would be coming back to Paris very soon.

'What is she doing, wandering around through Spain alone?' asked Giovanni.

'She likes to travel,' I said.

'Oh,' said Giovanni, 'nobody likes to travel, especially not women. There must be some other reason.' He raised his eyebrows suggestively. 'Perhaps she has a Spanish lover and is afraid to tell you – ? Perhaps she is with a *torero*.'

Perhaps she is, I thought. 'But she wouldn't be afraid to tell me.'

Giovanni laughed. 'I do not understand Americans at all,' he said.

'I don't see that there's anything very hard to understand. We aren't married, you know.'

'But she is your mistress, no?' asked Giovanni.

'Yes.'

'And she is still your mistress?'

I stared at him. 'Of course,' I said.

'Well then,' said Giovanni, 'I do not understand what she is doing in Spain while you are in Paris.' Another thought struck him. 'How old is she?'

'She's two years younger than I am.' I watched him. 'What's that got to do with it?'

'Is she married? I mean to somebody else, naturally.'

I laughed. He laughed too. 'Of course not.'

'Well, I thought she might be an older woman,' said Giovanni, 'with a husband somewhere and perhaps she had to go away with him from time to time in order to be able to continue her affair with you. That would be a nice arrangement. Those women are sometimes *very* interesting and they usually have a little money. If *that* woman was in Spain, she would bring back a wonderful gift for you. But a young girl, bouncing around in a foreign country by herself – I do not like that at all. You should find another mistress.'

It all seemed very funny. I could not stop laughing. 'Do *you* have a mistress?' I asked him.

'Not now,' he said, 'but perhaps I will again one day.' He half frowned, half smiled. 'I don't seem to be very interested in women right now – I don't know why. I used to be. Perhaps I will be again.' He shrugged. 'Perhaps it is because women are just a little more trouble than I can afford right now. *Et puis*' – He stopped.

I wanted to say that it seemed to me that he had taken a most peculiar road out of his trouble; but I only said, after a moment, cautiously: 'You don't seem to have a very high opinion of women.'

'Oh, women! There is no need, thank heaven, to have an opinion about *women*. Women are like water. They are tempting like that, and they can be that treacherous, and they can seem to be that bottomless, you know? – and they can be that shallow. And that dirty.' He stopped. 'I perhaps don't like women very much, that's true. That hasn't stopped me from making love to many and loving one or two. But most of the time – most of the time I made love only with the body.'

'That can make one very lonely,' I said. I had not expected to say it.

He had not expected to hear it. He looked at me and reached out and touched me on the cheek. 'Yes,' he said. Then 'I am not trying to be *méchant* when I talk about women. I respect women – very much – for their inside life, which is not like the life of a man.'

'Women don't seem to like that idea,' I said.

'Oh, well,' said Giovanni, 'these absurd women running around today, full of ideas and nonsense, and thinking themselves equal to men – *quelle rigolade*! – they need to be beaten half to death so that they can find out who rules the world.'

I laughed. 'Did the women you knew like to get beaten?'

He smiled. 'I don't know if they liked it. But a beating never made them go away.' We both laughed. 'They were not, any way, like that silly little girl of yours, wandering all over Spain and sending postcards back to Paris. What does she think she is doing? Does she want you or does she not want you?'

'She went to Spain,' I said, 'to find out.'

Giovanni opened his eyes wide. He was indignant. 'To Spain. Why not to China? What is she doing, testing all the Spaniards and comparing them with you?'

I was a little annoyed. 'You don't understand,' I said. 'She is a very intelligent, very complex girl, she wanted to go away and think.'

'What is there to think about? She sounds rather silly, I must say. She just can't make up her mind what bed to sleep in. She wants to eat her cake and she wants to have it all.'

'If she were in Paris now,' I said, abruptly, 'then I would not be in this room with you.'

'You would possibly not be living here,' he conceded, 'but we would certainly be seeing each other, why not?'

'Why *not*? Suppose she found out?'

'Found *out*? Found out what?'

'Oh stop it,' I said. 'You know what there is to find out.'

He looked at me very soberly. 'She sounds more and more impossible, this little girl of yours. What does she do, follow you everywhere? Or will she hire detectives to sleep under our bed? And what business is it of hers, anyway?'

'You can't possibly be serious,' I said.

'I certainly can be,' he retorted, 'and I am. You are the incomprehensible one.' He groaned and poured more coffee and picked up our cognac from the floor. '*Chez toi* everything sounds extremely feverish and complicated, like one of those English murder mysteries. To find out, to find out, you keep saying, as though we were accomplices in a crime. We have not committed any crime.' He poured the cognac.

'It's just that she'll be terribly hurt if she does find out, that's all. People have very dirty words for – for this situation.' I stopped. His face suggested that my reasoning was flimsy. I added, defensively 'Besides, it *is* a crime – in my country, and, after all, I didn't grow up here, I grew up *there*.'

'If dirty words frighten you,' said Giovanni, 'I really do not know how you have managed to live so long. People are full of dirty words. The only time they do not use them, most people I mean, is when they are describing something dirty.' He paused and we watched each other. In spite of what he was saying he looked rather frightened himself. 'If your countrymen think that privacy is a crime, so much the worse for your country. And as for this girl of yours – are you always at her side when she is here? I mean, all day, every day? You go out sometimes to have a drink alone, no? Maybe you sometimes take a walk without her – to think, as you say. The Americans seem to do a great deal of thinking. And perhaps while you are thinking and having that drink, you look at another girl who passes, no? Maybe you even look up at the sky and feel your own blood in you? Or does everything stop when Hella comes? No drinks alone, no looks at other girls, no sky? Eh? Answer me.'

'I've told you already that we're not married. But I don't seem to be able to make you understand anything at all this morning.'

'But anyway – when Hella is here you do sometimes see other people – without Hella?'

'Of course.'

'And does she make you tell her everything you have done while you were not with her?'

I sighed. I had lost control of the conversation somewhere along the line and I simply wanted it to end. I drank my cognac too fast and it burned my throat. 'Of course not.'

'Well. You are a very charming and good-looking and civilized boy and, unless you are impotent, I do not see what she has to complain about, or what you have to worry about. To arrange, *mon cher, la vie pratique*, is very simple – it only has to be done.' He reflected. 'Sometimes things go wrong, I agree, then you have to arrange it another way. But it is certainly not the English melodrama you make it. Why, that way, life would simply be unbearable.' He poured more cognac and grinned at me, as though he had solved all my problems. And there was something so artless in this smile that I had to smile back. Giovanni liked to believe that he was hard-headed and that I was not and that he was teaching me the stony facts of life. It was very important for him to feel this: it was because he knew, unwillingly, at the very bottom of his heart, that I helplessly, at the very bottom of mine, resisted him with all my strength.

Eventually we grew still, we fell silent, and we slept. We awoke around three or four in the afternoon, when the dull sun was prying at odd corners of the cluttered room. We arose and washed and shaved, bumping into each other and making jokes and furious with the unstated desire to escape the room. Then we danced out into the streets, into Paris, and ate quickly somewhere, and I left Giovanni at the door to Guillaume's bar.

Then I, alone, and relieved to be alone, perhaps went to a movie, or walked, or returned home and read, or sat in a park and read, or sat on a cafe terrace, or talked to people, or wrote letters. I wrote to Hella, telling her nothing, or I wrote to my father asking for money. And no matter what I was doing, another me sat in my belly, absolutely cold with terror over the question of my life.

Giovanni had awakened an itch, had released a gnaw in me. I realized it one afternoon, when I was taking him to work via the boulevard Montparnasse. We had bought a kilo of cherries and we were eating them as we walked along. We were both insufferably childish and high-spirited that afternoon and the spectacle we presented, two grown men, jostling each other on the wide sidewalk, and aiming the cherry-pips, as though they were spitballs, into each other's faces, must have been outrageous. And I realized that such childishness was fantastic at my age and the happiness out of which it sprang yet more so; for that moment I really loved Giovanni, who had never seemed more beautiful than he was that afternoon. And, watching his face, I realized that it meant much to me that I could make his face so bright. I saw that I might be willing to give a great deal not to lose that power. And I felt myself flow toward him, as a river rushes when the ice breaks up. Yet, at that very moment, there passed between us on the pavement another boy, a stranger, and I invested him at once with Giovanni's beauty and what I felt for Giovanni I also felt for him. Giovanni saw this and saw my face and it made him laugh the more. I blushed and he kept laughing and then the boulevard, the light, the sound of his laughter turned into a scene from a nightmare. I kept looking at the trees, the light falling through the leaves. I felt sorrow and shame and panic and great bitterness. At the same time – it was part of my turmoil and also outside it – I felt the muscles in my neck tighten with the effort I was making not to turn my head and watch that boy diminish down the bright avenue. The beast which Giovanni had awakened in me would never go to sleep again; but one day I would not be with Giovanni any more. And would I then, like all the others, find myself turning and following all kinds of boys down God knows what dark avenues, into what dark places?

With this fearful intimation there opened in me a hatred for Giovanni which was as powerful as my love and which was nourished by the same roots.

2

I scarcely know how to describe that room. It became, in a way, every room I had ever been in and every room I find myself in hereafter will remind me of Giovanni's room. I did not really stay there very long – we met before the spring began and I left there during the summer – but it still seems to me that I spent a lifetime there. Life in that room seemed to be occurring underwater, as I say, and it is certain that I underwent a sea-change there.

To begin with, the room was not large enough for two, it looked out on a small courtyard. 'Looked out' means only that the room had two windows, against which the court-yard malevolently pressed, encroaching day by day, as though it had confused itself with a jungle. We, or rather Giovanni, kept the windows closed most of the time; he had never bought any curtains, neither did we buy any while I was in the room; to insure privacy, Giovanni had obscured the window panes with a heavy, white cleaning polish. We sometimes heard children playing outside our window, sometimes strange shapes loomed against it. At such moments, Giovanni, working in the room, or lying in the bed, would stiffen like a hunting dog and remain perfectly silent until whatever seemed to threaten our safety had moved away.

He had always had great plans for remodelling this room and before I arrived he had already begun. One of the walls was a dirty, streaked white where he had torn off the wallpaper. The wall facing it was destined never to be uncovered and on this wall a lady in a hoop skirt and a man in knee breeches perpetually walked together, hemmed in by roses. The wallpaper lay on the floor, in great sheets and scrolls, in dust. On the floor also, lay our dirty laundry, along with Giovanni's tools and the paint brushes and the bottles of oil and turpentine. Our suitcases teetered on top of something, so that

76

we dreaded ever having to open them and sometimes went without some minor necessity, such as clean socks, for days.

No one ever came to see us, except Jacques, and he did not come often. We were far from the center of the city and we had no phone.

I remember the first afternoon I woke up there, with Giovanni fast asleep beside me, heavy as a fallen rock. The sun filtered through the room so faintly that I was worried about the time. I stealthily lit a cigarette, for I did not want to wake Giovanni. I did not yet know how I would face his eyes. I looked about me. Giovanni had said something in the taxi about his room being very dirty. 'I'm sure it is,' I had said lightly, and turned away from him, looking out of the window. Then we had both been silent. When I woke up in his room, I remembered that there had been something strained and painful in the quality of that silence; which had been broken when Giovanni said, with a shy, bitter smile: 'I must find some poetic figure.'

And he spread his heavy fingers in the air, as though a metaphor were tangible. I watched him.

'Look at the garbage of this city,' he said, finally, and his fingers indicated the flying street, 'all of the garbage of this city? Where do they take it? I don't know where they take it – but it might very well be my room.'

'It's much more likely,' I said, 'that they dump it into the Seine.'

But I sensed, when I woke up and looked around the room, the bravado and the cowardice of his figure of speech. This was not the garbage of Paris, which would have been anonymous: this was Giovanni's regurgitated life.

Before and beside me and all over the room, towering like a wall, were boxes of cardboard and leather, some tied with string, some locked, some bursting, and out of the topmost box before me spilled down sheets of violin music. There was a violin in the room, lying on the table in its warped, cracked case – it was impossible to guess from looking at it whether it had been laid to rest there yesterday or a hundred years before. The table was loaded with yellowing newspapers and empty bottles and it held a single brown and wrinkled potato in which even the sprouting eyes were rotten. Red wine had been spilled on the floor, it had been allowed to dry and it made the air in the room sweet and heavy. But it was not the room's disorder which was frightening; it was the fact that when one began searching for the key to this disorder one realized that it was not to be found in any of the usual places. For this was not a matter of habit or circumstances or temperament; it was a matter of punishment and grief. I do not know how I knew this, but I knew it at once; perhaps I knew it because I wanted to live. And I stared at the room with the same nervous, calculating extension of the intelligence and of all one's forces which occur when gauging a mortal and unavoidable danger: at the silent walls of the room with its distant, archaic lovers trapped in an interminable rose garden, and the staring windows, staring like two great eyes of ice and fire, and the ceiling which lowered like those clouds out of which fiends have sometimes spoken and which obscured but failed to soften its malevolence behind the yellow light which hung like a diseased and undefinable sex in its center. Under this blunted arrow, this smashed flower of light lay the terrors which encompassed Giovanni's soul. I understood why Giovanni had wanted me and had brought me to his last retreat. I was to destroy this room and give to Giovanni a new and better life. This life could only be my own, which, in order to transform Giovanni's, must first become a part of Giovanni's room.

In the beginning, because the motives which led me to Giovanni's room were so mixed; had so little to do with his hopes and desires and were so deeply a part of my own desperation, I invented in myself a kind of pleasure in playing the housewife after Giovanni had gone to work. I threw out the paper, the bottles, the fantastic accumulation of trash, I examined the contents of the innumerable boxes and suitcases, and disposed of them. But I am not a housewife – men never can be housewives. And the pleasure was never real or deep, though Giovanni smiled his humble, grateful smile and told me in as many ways as he could find how wonderful it was to have me there, how I stood, with my love and my ingenuity, between him and the dark. Each day he invited me to witness how he had changed, how love had changed him, how he worked and sang and cherished me. I was in a terrible confusion. Sometimes I thought, but this *is* your life. Stop fighting it. Stop fighting. Or I thought, but I am happy. And he loves me. I am safe. Sometimes, when he was not near me, I thought, I will never let him touch me again. Then, when he touched me, I thought it doesn't matter, it is only the body, it will soon be over. When it was over I lay in the dark and listened to his breathing and dreamed of the touch of hands, of Giovanni's hands, or anybody's hands, hands which would have the power to crush me and make me whole again.

Sometimes I left Giovanni over our afternoon breakfast, blue smoke from a cigarette circling around his head, and went off to the American Express Office at Opéra, where my mail would be, if I had any. Sometimes, but rarely, Giovanni came with me; he said that he could not endure being surrounded by so many Americans. He said they all looked alike – as I am sure they did, to him. But they didn't look alike to me. I was aware that they all had in common something that made them Americans but I could never put my finger on what it was. I knew that whatever this common quality was, I shared it. And I knew that Giovanni had been attracted to me partly because of it. When Giovanni wanted me to know that he was displeased with me, he said I was a '*vrai americain*'; conversely, when delighted, he said that I was not an American at all; and on both occasions he was striking, deep in me, a nerve which did not throb in him. And I resented this: resented being called an American (and resented resenting it) because it seemed to make me nothing more than that, whatever that was; and I resented being called *not* an American because it seemed to make me nothing.

Yet, walking into the American Express Office one harshly bright, midsummer afternoon, I was forced to admit that this active, so disquietingly cheerful horde struck the eye, at once, as a unit. At home, I could have distinguished patterns, habits, accents of speech – with no effort whatever; now everybody sounded, unless I listened hard, as though they had just arrived from Nebraska. At home I could have seen the clothes they were wearing, but here I only saw bags, cameras, belts and hats, all, clearly, from the same department store. At home I would have had some sense of the individual womanhood of the woman I faced: here the most ferociously accomplished seemed to be involved in some ice-cold or sun-dried travesty of sex, and even grandmothers seemed to have had no traffic with the flesh. And what distinguished the men was that they seemed incapable of age; they smelled of soap, which seemed indeed to be their preservative against the dangers and exigencies of any more intimate odor; the boy he had been shone somehow, unsoiled, untouched, unchanged, through the eye of the man of sixty, booking passage, with his smiling wife, to Rome. His wife might have been his mother, forcing more oatmeal down his throat, and Rome might have been the movie she had promised to allow him to see. Yet I also suspected that what I was seeing was but a part of the truth and perhaps not even the most important part; beneath these faces, these clothes, accents, rudenesses, was power and sorrow, both unadmitted, unrealized, the power of inventors, the sorrow of the disconnected.

I took my place in the mail line behind two girls who had decided that they wanted to stay on in Europe and who were hoping to find jobs with the American government in Germany. One of them had fallen in love with a Swiss boy; so I gathered, from the low, intense, and troubled conversation she was having with her friend. The friend was urging her to 'put her foot down' – on what principle I could not discover: and the girl in love kept nodding her head, but more in perplexity than agreement. She had the choked and halting air of someone who has something more to say but finds no way of saying it. 'You mustn't be a fool about this,' the friend was saying. 'I know, I know,' said the girl. One had the impression that, though she certainly did not wish to be a fool, she had lost one definition of the word and might never be able to find another.

There were two letters for me, one from my father and one from Hella. Hella had been sending me only postcards for quite awhile. I was afraid her letter might be important and I did not want to read it. I opened the letter from my father first. I read it, standing just beyond reach of the sunlight, beside the endlessly swinging double doors.

'*Dear Butch*,' my father said, '*aren't you ever coming home? Don't you think I'm only being selfish but it's true I'd like to see you. I think you have been away long enough, God knows I don't know what you're doing over there, and you don't write enough for me even to guess. But my guess is you're going to be sorry one of these fine days that you stayed over there, looking at your navel, and let the world pass you by. There's nothing over there for you. You're as American as pork and beans, though maybe you don't want to think so any more. And maybe you won't mind my saying that you're getting a little old for studying, after all, if that's what you're doing. You're pushing thirty. I'm getting along, too, and you're all I've got. I'd like to see you.*

'*You keep asking me to send you your money and I guess you think I'm being a bastard about it. I'm not trying to starve you out and you know if you really need anything, I'll be the first to help you but I really don't think I'd be doing you a favor by letting you spend what little money you've got over there and then coming home to nothing. What the hell are you doing? Let your old man in on the secret, can't you? You may not believe this, but once I was a young man, too.*'

And then he went on about my stepmother and how she wanted to see me, and about some of our friends and what they were doing. It was clear that my absence was beginning to frighten him. He did not know what it meant. But he was living, obviously, in a pit of suspicions which daily became blacker and vaguer – he would not have known how to put them into words, even if he had dared. The question he longed to ask was not in the letter and neither was the offer: *Is it a woman, David? Bring her on home. I don't care who she is. Bring her on home and I'll help you get set up.* He could not risk this question because he could not have endured the answer in the negative. An answer in the negative would have revealed what strangers we had become. I folded the letter and put it in my back pocket and looked out for a moment at the wide, sunlit foreign avenue.

There was a sailor, dressed all in white, coming across the boulevard, walking with that funny roll sailors have and with that aura, hopeful and hard, of having to make a great deal happen in a hurry. I was staring at him, though I did not know it, and wishing I were he. He seemed – somehow – younger than I had ever been, and blonder and more beautiful, and he wore his masculinity as unequivocally as he wore his skin. He made me think of home – perhaps home is not a place but simply an irrevocable condition. I knew how he drank and how he was with his friends and how pain and women baffled him. I wondered if my father had ever been like that, if I had ever been like that – though it was hard to imagine, for this boy, striding across the avenue like light itself, any antecedents, any connections at all. We came abreast and, as though he had seen some all-revealing panic in my eyes, he gave me a look contemptuously lewd and knowing; just such a look as he might have given, but a few hours ago, to the desperately well-dressed nymphomaniac or trollop who was trying to make him believe she was a lady. And in another second, had our contact lasted, I was certain that there would erupt into speech, out of all that light and beauty, some brutal variation of *Look, baby. I know you.* I felt my face flame, I felt my heart harden and shake as I hurried past him, trying to look stonily beyond him. He had caught me by surprise, for I had, somehow, not really been thinking of him but of the letter in my pocket, of Hella and Giovanni. I got to the other side of the boulevard, not daring to look back, and I wondered what he had seen in me to elicit such instantaneous contempt. I was too old to suppose that it had anything to do with my walk, or the way I held my hands, or my voice – which, anyway, he had not heard. It was something else and I would never see it. I would never dare to see it. It would be like looking at the naked sun. But, hurrying, and not daring now to look at anyone, male or female, who passed me on the wide sidewalks, I knew that what the sailor had seen in my unguarded eyes was envy and desire: I had seen it often in Jacques' eyes and my reaction and the sailor's had been the same. But if I were still able to feel affection and if he had seen it in my eyes, it would not have helped, for affection, for the boys I was doomed to look at, was vastly more frightening than lust.

I walked further than I had intended, for I did not dare to stop while the sailor might still be watching. Near the river, on rue des Pyramides, I sat down at a cafe table and opened Hella's letter.

Mon cher, she began, *Spain is my favorite country* mais ça n'empêche que Paris est toujours ma ville preferé. *I long to be again among all those foolish people, running for metros and jumping off of buses and dodging motorcycles and having traffic jams and admiring all that crazy statuary in all those absurd parks. I weep for the fishy ladies in the place de la Concorde. Spain is not like that at all. Whatever else Spain is, it is not frivolous. I think, really, that I would stay in Spain forever – if I had never been to Paris. Spain is very beautiful, stony and sunny and lonely. But by and by you get tired of olive oil and fish and castanets and tambourines – or, anyway, I do. I want to come home, to come home to Paris. It's funny, I've never felt anyplace was home before.*

Nothing has happened to me here – I suppose that pleases you, I confess it rather pleases me. The Spaniards are nice, but, of course, most of them are terribly poor, the ones who aren't are impossible, I don't like the tourists, mainly English and American dipsomaniacs, paid, my dear, by their families to stay away. (I wish I had a family.) I'm on Mallorca now and it would be a pretty place if you could dump all the pensioned widows into the sea and make dry-martini drinking illegal. I've never seen anything like it! The way these old hags guzzle and make eyes at anything in pants, especially anything about eighteen – well, I said to myself, Hella, my girl, take a good look. You may be looking at your future. The trouble is that I love myself too much. And so I've decided to let two try it, this business of loving me, I mean, and see how that works out. (I feel fine now that I've made the decision, I hope you'll feel fine, too, dear knight in Gimbel's armor.)

I've been trapped into some dreary expedition to Seville with an English family I met in Barcelona. They adore Spain and they want to take me to see a bull-fight – I never have, you know, all the time I've been wandering around here. They're really quite nice, he's some kind of poet with the B.B.C. and she's his efficient and adoring spouse. Quite nice, really. They do have an impossibly lunatick son who imagines himself mad about me, but he's much too English and much,

much too young. I leave tomorrow and shall be gone ten days. Then, they to England and I – to you!

I folded this letter, which I now realized I had been awaiting for many days and nights, and the waiter came and asked me what I wanted to drink. I had meant to order an aperitif but now, in some grotesque spirit of celebration, ordered a Scotch and soda. And over this drink, which had never seemed more American than it did at that moment, I stared at absurd Paris, which was as cluttered now, under the scalding sun, as the landscape of my heart. I wondered what I was going to do.

I cannot say that I was frightened. Or, it would be better to say that I did not feel any fear – the way men who are shot do not, I am told, feel any pain for awhile. I felt a certain relief. It seemed that the necessity for decision had been taken from my hands. I told myself that we both had always known, Giovanni and myself, that our idyll could not last forever. And it was not as though I had not been honest with him – he knew all about Hella. He knew that she would be returning to Paris one day. Now she would be coming back and my life with Giovanni would be finished. It would be something that had happened to many men once. I paid for my drink and got up and walked across the river to Montparnasse.

I felt elated – yet, as I walked down Raspail toward the cafes of Montparnasse, I could not fail to remember that Hella and I had walked here, Giovanni and I had walked here. And with each step, the face that glowed insistently before me was not her face, but his. I was beginning to wonder how he would take my news. I did not think he would fight me but I was afraid of what I would see in his face. I was afraid of the pain I would see there. But even this was not my real fear. My real fear was buried and was driving me to Montparnasse. I wanted to find a girl, any girl at all.

But the terraces seemed oddly deserted. I walked along slowly, on both sides of the street, looking at the tables. I saw no one I knew. I walked down as far as the *Closerie des Lilas* and I had a solitary drink there. I read my letters again. I thought of finding Giovanni at once and telling him I was leaving him but I knew he would not yet have opened the bar and he might be almost anywhere in Paris at this hour. I walked slowly back up the boulevard. Then I saw a couple of girls, French whores, but they were not very attractive. I told myself that I could do better than *that*. I got to the *Select* and sat down. I watched the people pass, and I drank. No one I knew appeared on the boulevard for the longest while.

The person who appeared, and whom I did not know very well, was a girl named Sue, blonde, and rather puffy, with the quality, in spite of the fact that she was not pretty, of the girls who are selected each year to be Miss Rheingold. She wore her curly blonde hair cut very short, she had small breasts and a big behind, and, in order, no doubt, to indicate to the world how little she cared for appearance or sensuality, she almost always wore tight blue jeans. I think she came from Philadelphia and her family was very rich. Sometimes, when she was drunk, she reviled them, and, sometimes, drunk in another way, she extolled their virtues of thrift and fidelity. I was both dismayed and relieved to see her. The moment she appeared I began, mentally, to take off all her clothes.

'Sit down,' I said. 'Have a drink.'

'I'm glad to *see* you,' she cried, sitting down, and looking about for the waiter. 'You'd rather dropped out of sight. How've you been?' – abandoning her search for the waiter and leaning forward to me with a friendly grin.

'I've been fine,' I told her. 'And you?'

'Oh, *me*! Nothing ever happens to me.' And she turned down the corners of her rather predatory and also vulnerable mouth to indicate that she was both joking and not joking. 'I'm built like a brick stonewall.' We both laughed. She peered at me. 'They tell me you're living way out at the end of Paris, near the zoo.'

'I found a maid's room out there. Very cheap.'

'Are you living alone?'

I did not know whether she knew about Giovanni or not. I felt a hint of sweat on my forehead. 'Sort of,' I said.

'Sort of? What the hell does *that* mean? Do you have a monkey with you, or something?'

I grinned. 'No. But this French kid I know, he lives with his mistress, but they fight a lot and it's really *his* room so sometimes, when his mistress throws him out, he bunks with me for a couple of days.'

'Ah!' she sighed. '*Chagrin d'amour!*'

'He's having a good time,' I said. 'He loves it.' I looked at her. 'Aren't you?'

'Stonewalls,' she said, 'are impenetrable.'

The waiter arrived. 'Doesn't it,' I dared, 'depend on the weapon?'

'What are you buying me to drink?' she asked.

'What do you want?' We were both grinning. The waiter stood above us, manifesting a kind of surly *joie de vivre*.

'I believe I'll have' – she batted the eyelashes of her tight blue eyes – '*un ricard*. With a hell of a lot of ice.'

'*Deux ricards,*' I said to the waiter, '*avec beaucoup de la glace.*'

'*Oui, monsieur.*' I was sure he despised us both. I thought of Giovanni and of how many times in an evening the phrase, *Oui monsieur* fell from his lips. With this fleeting thought there came another, equally fleeting: a new sense of Giovanni, his private life and pain, and all that moved like a flood in him when we lay together at night.

'To continue,' I said.

'To continue?' She made her eyes very wide and blank. 'Where were we?' She was trying to be coquettish and she was trying to be hard-headed. I felt that I was doing something very cruel.

But I could not stop. 'We were talking about stonewalls and how they could be entered.'

'I never knew,' she simpered, 'that you had any interest in stonewalls.'

'There's a lot about me you don't know.' The waiter returned with our drinks. 'Don't you think discoveries are fun?'

She stared discontentedly at her drink. 'Frankly,' she said, turning toward me again, with those eyes, 'no.'

'Oh you're much too young for that,' I said. '*Everything* should be a discovery.'

She was silent for a moment. She sipped her drink. 'I've made,' she said, finally, 'all the discoveries that I can stand.' But I watched the way her thighs moved against the cloth of her jeans.

'But you can't just go on being a brick stonewall forever.'

'I don't see why not,' she said. 'Nor do I see *how* not.'

'Baby,' I said, 'I'm making you a proposition.'

She picked up her glass again and sipped it, staring straight outward at the boulevard. 'And what's the proposition?'

'Invite me for a drink. *Chez toi.*'

'I don't believe,' she said, turning to me, 'that I've got anything in the house.'

'We can pick up something on the way,' I said.

She stared at me for a long time. I forced myself not to drop my eyes. 'I'm sure that I shouldn't,' she said at last.

'Why not?'

She made a small, helpless movement in the wicker chair. 'I don't know. I don't know what you want.'

I laughed. 'If you invite me home for a drink,' I said, 'I'll show you.'

'I think you're being impossible,' she said, and for the first time there was something genuine in her eyes and voice.

'Well,' I said, 'I think *you* are.' I looked at her with a smile which was, I hoped, both boyish and insistent. 'I don't know what I've said that's so impossible. I've put all my cards on the table. But you're still holding yours. I don't know why you should think a man's being impossible when he declares himself attracted to you.'

'Oh, please,' she said, and finished her drink, 'I'm sure it's just the summer sun.'

'The summer sun,' I said, 'has nothing to do with it.' And when she still made no answer, 'All you've got to do,' I said, desperately, 'is decide whether we'll have another drink here or at your place.'

She snapped her fingers abruptly and did not succeed in appearing jaunty. 'Come along,' she said, 'I'm certain to regret it. But you really will have to buy something to drink. There *isn't* anything in the house. And that way,' she added, after a moment, 'I'll be sure to get something out of the deal.'

It was I, then, who felt a dreadful holding back. To avoid looking at her, I made a great show of getting the waiter. And he came, as surly as ever, and I paid him, and we rose and started walking toward the rue de Sèvres, where Sue had a small apartment.

Her apartment was dark and full of furniture. 'None of it is mine,' she said. 'It all belongs to the French lady of a certain age from whom I rented it, who is now in Monte Carlo for her nerves.' She was very nervous, too, and I saw that this nervousness could be, for a little while, a great help to me. I had bought a small bottle of cognac and I put it down on her marble-topped table and took her in my arms. For some reason I was terribly aware that it was after seven in the evening, that soon the sun would have disappeared from the river, that all the Paris night was about to begin, and that Giovanni was now at work.

She was very big and she was disquietingly fluid – fluid, without, however, being able to flow. I felt a hardness and a constriction in her, a grave distrust, created already by too many men like me, ever to be conquered now. What we were about to do would not be pretty.

And, as though she felt this, she moved away from me. 'Let's have a drink,' she said. 'Unless of course, you're in a hurry. I'll try not to keep you any longer than absolutely necessary.'

She smiled and I smiled, too. We were as close in that instant as we would ever get – like two thieves. 'Let's have several drinks,' I said.

'But not *too* many,' she said, and simpered again, suggestively, like a broken-down movie queen facing the cruel cameras again after a long eclipse.

She took the cognac and disappeared into her corner of a kitchen. 'Make yourself comfortable,' she shouted out to me. 'Take off your shoes. Take off your socks. Look at my books – I often wonder what I'd do if there weren't any books in the world.'

I took off my shoes and lay back on her sofa. I tried not to think. But I was thinking that what I did with Giovanni could not possibly be more immoral than what I was about to do with Sue.

She came back with two great brandy snifters. She came close to me on the sofa and we touched glasses. We drank a little, she watching me all the while, and then I touched her breasts. Her lips parted and she put her glass down with extraordinary clumsiness and lay against me. It was a gesture of great despair and I knew that she was giving herself, not to me, but to that lover who would never come.

And I – I thought of many things, lying coupled with Sue in that dark place. I wondered if she had done anything to prevent herself from becoming pregnant; and the thought of a child belonging to Sue and me, of my being trapped that way – in the very act, so to speak, of trying to escape – almost precipitated a laughing jag. I wondered if her blue jeans had been thrown on top of the cigarette she had been smoking. I wondered if anyone else had a key to her apartment, if we could be heard through the inadequate walls, how much, in a few moments, we would hate each other. I also approached Sue as though she were a job of work, a job which it was necessary to do in an unforgettable manner. Somewhere, at the very bottom of myself, I realized that I was doing something awful to her and it became a matter of my honor not to let this fact become too obvious. I tried to convey, through this grisly act of love, the intelligence, at least, that it was not her, not *her* flesh, that I despised – it would not be her I could not face when we became vertical again. Again, somewhere at the bottom of me, I realized that my fears had been excessive and groundless and, in effect, a lie: it became clearer every instant that what I had been afraid of had nothing to do with my body. Sue was not Hella and she did not lessen my terror of what would happen when Hella came: she increased it, she made it more real than it had been before. At the same time, I realized that my performance with Sue was succeeding even too well, and I tried not to despise her for feeling so little what her laborer felt. I travelled through a network of Sue's cries, of Sue's tom-tom fists on my back, and judged, by means of her thighs, by means of her legs, how soon I could be free. Then I thought, *The end is coming soon*, her sobs became even higher and harsher, I was terribly aware of the small of my back and the cold sweat there. I thought *Well let her have it for Christ sake, get it over with*, then it was ending and I hated her and me, then it was over, and the dark, tiny room rushed back. And I wanted only to get out of there.

She lay still for a long time. I felt the night outside and it was calling me. I leaned up at last and found a cigarette.

'Perhaps,' she said, 'we should finish our drinks.'

She sat up and switched on the lamp which stood beside her bed. I had been dreading this moment. But she saw nothing in my eyes – she stared at me as though I had made a long journey on a white charger all the way to her prison house. She lifted her glass.

'*A la votre*,' I said.

'*A la* votre?' She giggled. '*A la* tienne, *chéri!*' She leaned over and kissed me on the mouth. Then, for a moment, she felt something; she leaned back and stared at me, her eyes not quite tightening yet; and she said, lightly, 'Do you suppose we could do this again sometime?'

'I don't see why not,' I told her, trying to laugh. 'We carry our own equipment.'

She was silent. Then: 'Could we have supper together – tonight?'

'I'm sorry,' I said. 'I'm really sorry, Sue, but I've got a date.'

'Oh. Tomorrow, maybe?'

'Look, Sue. I hate to make dates. I'll just surprise you.'

She finished her drink. 'I doubt that,' she said. She got up and walked away from me. 'I'll just put on some clothes and come down with you.'

She disappeared and I heard the water running. I sat there, still naked, but with my socks on, and poured myself another brandy. Now I was afraid to go out into that night which had seemed to be calling me only a few moments before.

When she came back she was wearing a dress and some real shoes, and she had sort of fluffed up her hair. I had to admit she looked better that way, really more like a girl, like a schoolgirl. I rose and started putting on my clothes. 'You look nice,' I said.

There were a great many things she wanted to say, but she forced herself to say nothing. I could scarcely bear to watch the struggle occurring in her face, it made me so ashamed. 'Maybe you'll be lonely again,' she said, finally. 'I guess I won't mind if you come looking for me.' She wore the strangest smile I had ever seen. It was pained and vindictive and humiliated but she inexpertly smeared across this grimace a bright, girlish gaiety – as rigid as the skeleton beneath her flabby body. If fate ever allowed Sue to reach me, she would kill me with just that smile.

'Keep a candle,' I said, 'in the window' – and she opened her door and we passed out into the streets.

3

I left her at the nearest corner, mumbling some schoolboy excuse, and watched her stolid figure cross the boulevard toward the cafes.

I did not know what to do or where to go. I found myself at last along the river, slowly going home.

And this was perhaps the first time in my life that death occurred to me as a reality. I thought of the people before me who had looked down at the river and gone to sleep beneath it. I wondered about them. I wondered how they had done it – it, the physical act. I had thought of suicide when I was much younger, as, possibly, we all have, but then it would have been for revenge, it would have been my way of informing the world how awfully it had made me suffer. But the silence of the evening, as I wandered home, had nothing to do with that storm, that far-off boy. I simply wondered about the dead because their days had ended and I did not know how I would get through mine.

The city, Paris, which I loved so much, was absolutely silent. There seemed to be almost no one on the streets, although it was still very early in the evening. Nevertheless, beneath me – along the river bank, beneath the bridges, in the shadow of the walls, I could almost hear the collective, shivering sigh – were lovers and ruins, sleeping, embracing, coupling, drinking, staring out at the descending night. Behind the walls of the houses I passed, the French nation was clearing away the dishes, putting little Jean Pierre and Marie to bed, scowling over the eternal problems of the sou, the shop, the church, the unsteady State. Those walls, those shuttered windows, held them in and protected them against the darkness and the long moan of this long night. Ten years hence, little Jean Pierre and Marie might find themselves out here beside the river and wonder, like me, how they had fallen out of the web of safety. What a long way, I thought, I've come – to be destroyed!

Yet it was true, I recalled, turning away from the river down the long street home, I wanted children. I wanted to be inside again, with the light and safety, with my manhood unquestioned, watching my woman put my children to bed. I wanted the same bed at night and the same arms and I wanted to rise in the morning, knowing where I was. I wanted a woman to be for me a steady ground, like the earth itself, where I could always be renewed. It had been so once; it had almost been so once. I could make it so again, I could make it real. It only demanded a short, hard strength for me to become myself again.

I saw a light burning beneath our door as I walked down the corridor. Before I put my key in the lock the door was opened from within. Giovanni stood there, his hair in his eyes, laughing. He held a glass of cognac in his hand. I was struck at first by what seemed to be the merriment on his face. Then I saw that it was not merriment but hysteria and despair.

I started to ask him what he was doing home, but he pulled me into the room, holding me around the neck tightly, with one hand. He was shaking. 'Where have you been?' I looked into his face, pulling slightly away from him. 'I have looked for you everywhere.'

'Didn't you go to work?' I asked him.

'No,' he said. 'Have a drink. I have bought a bottle of cognac to celebrate my freedom.' He poured me a cognac. I did not seem to be able to move. He came toward me again, thrusting the glass into my hand.

'Giovanni – what happened?'

He did not answer. He suddenly sat down on the edge of the bed, bent over. I saw then that he was also in a state of rage. '*Ils sont sale, les gens, tu sais?*' He looked up at me. His eyes were full of tears. 'They are just dirty, all of them, low and cheap and dirty.' He stretched out his hand and pulled me down to the floor beside him. 'All except you. *Tous, sauf toi.*' He held my face between his hands and I suppose such tenderness has scarcely ever produced such terror as I then felt. '*Ne me laisse pas tomber, je t'en prie,*' he said, and kissed me, with strange insistent gentleness on the mouth.

His touch could never fail to make me feel desire; yet his hot, sweet breath also made me want to vomit. I pulled away as gently as I could and drank my cognac. 'Giovanni,' I said, 'please tell me what happened. What's the matter?'

'He fired me,' he said. 'Guillaume. *Il m'a mis à la porte.*' He laughed and rose and began walking up and down the tiny room. 'He told me never to come to his bar any more. He said I was a gangster and a thief and a dirty little street boy and the only reason I ran after him – *I* ran after *him* – was because I intended to rob him one night. *Après l'amour. Merde!*' He laughed again.

I could not say anything. I felt that the walls of the room were closing in on me.

Giovanni stood in front of our whitewashed windows, his back to me. 'He said all these things in front of many people, right downstairs in the bar. He waited until people came. I wanted to kill him, I wanted to kill them all.' He turned back into the center of the room and poured himself another cognac. He drank it at a breath, then suddenly took his glass and hurled it with all his strength against the wall. It rang briefly and fell in a thousand pieces all over our bed, all over the floor. I could not move at once; then, feeling that my feet were being held back by water but also watching myself move very fast, I grabbed him by the shoulders. He began to cry. I held him. And, while I felt his anguish entering into me, like acid in his sweat, and felt that my heart would burst for him, I also wondered, with an unwilling, unbelieving contempt, why I had ever thought him strong.

He pulled away from me and sat against the wall which had been uncovered. I sat facing him.

'I arrived at the usual time,' he said. 'I felt very good today. He was not there when I arrived and I cleaned the bar as usual and had a little drink and a little something to eat. Then he came and I could see at once that he was in a dangerous mood – perhaps he had just been humiliated by some young boy. It is funny' – and he smiled – 'you can tell when Guillaume is in a dangerous mood because he then becomes so respectable. When something has happened to humiliate him and make him see, even for a moment, how disgusting he is, and how alone, then he remembers that he

is a member of one of the best and oldest families in France. But
maybe, then, he remembers that his name is going to die with him.
Then he has to do something, quick, to make the feeling go away.
He has to make much noise or have some *very* pretty boy or get
drunk or have a fight or look at his dirty pictures.' He paused and
stood up and began walking up and down again. 'I do not know
what happened to him today, but when he came in he tried at first
to be very business-like – he was trying to find fault with my work.
But there was nothing wrong and he went upstairs. Then by and
by, he called me. I hate going up to that little *pied-à-terre* he has
up there over the bar, it always means a scene. But I had to go and
I found him in his dressing gown, covered with perfume. I do not
know why, but the moment I saw him like that, I began to be
angry. He looked at me as though he were some fabulous coquette
– and he is ugly, ugly, he has a body just like sour milk! – and then
he asked me how you were. I was a little astonished, for he never
mentions you. I said you were fine. He asked me if we still lived
together. I think perhaps I should have lied to him but I did not
see any reason to lie to such a disgusting old fairy, so I said, *Bien
sûr*. I was trying to be calm. Then he asked me terrible questions
and I began to get sick watching him and listening to him. I
thought it was best to be very quick with him and I said that such
questions were not asked, even by a priest or a doctor, and I said
he should be ashamed. Maybe he had been waiting for me to say
something like that, for then he became angry and he reminded
me that he had taken me out of the streets, *et il a fait ceci et il a fait
cela*, everything for me because he thought I was adorable, *parce-qu'il
m'adorait* – and on and on and that I had no gratitude and no decency.
I maybe handled it all very badly, I know how I would have done
it even a few months ago, I would have made him scream, I would
have made him kiss my feet, *je te jure*! – but I did not want to do
that, I really did not want to be dirty with him. I tried to be serious.
I told him that I had never told him any lies and I had always said
that I did not want to be lovers with him – and – he had given me
the job all the same. I said I worked very hard and was very honest
with him and that it was not my fault if – if I did not feel for him

as he felt for me. Then he reminded me that once – one time – and I did not want to say yes, but I was weak from hunger and had trouble not to vomit. I was still trying to be calm and trying to handle it right. So I said, *Mais a ce moment là je n'avais pas un copain.* I am not alone any more, *je suis avec un gars maintenant.* I thought he would understand that, he is very fond of romance and the dream of fidelity. But not this time. He laughed and said a few more awful things about you, and he said that you were an American boy, after all, doing things in France which you would not dare to do at home, and that you would leave me very soon. Then, at last, I got angry and I said that he did not pay me a salary for listening to slander and then I heard someone come into the bar downstairs so I turned around without saying anything more and walked out.'

He stopped in front of me. 'Can I have some more cognac?' he asked, with a smile. 'I won't break the glass this time.'

I gave him my glass. He emptied it and handed it back. He watched my face. 'Don't be afraid,' he said. 'We will be alright. I am not afraid.' Then his eyes darkened, he looked again toward the windows.

'Well,' he said, 'I hoped that that would be the end of it. I worked in the bar and tried not to think of Guillaume or of what he was thinking or doing upstairs. It was aperitif time, you know? and I was very busy. Then, suddenly I heard the door slam upstairs and the moment I heard that I knew that it had happened, the awful thing had happened. He came into the bar, all dressed now, like a French business man, and came straight to me. He did not speak to anyone as he came in, and he looked white and angry and, naturally, this attracted attention. Everyone was waiting to see what he would do. And, I must say, I thought he was going to strike me, or he had maybe gone mad and had a pistol in his pocket. So I am sure I looked frightened and this did not help matters, either. He came behind the bar and began saying that I was a *tapette* and a thief and told me to leave at once or he would call the police and have me put behind bars. I was so astonished I could not say anything and all the time his voice was rising and people were beginning to listen and, suddenly, *mon cher*, I felt that I was falling, falling from a great, high place. For a long while I could not get angry and I could feel the tears, like fire, coming up. I could not get my breath, I could not *believe* that he was really doing this to me. I kept saying, what have I done? What have I *done*? And he would not answer and then he shouted, very loud, it was like a gun going off, *'Mais tu le sais, salop!'* You know very well! And nobody knew what he meant, but it was just as though we were back in that theatre lobby again, where we met, you remember? Everybody knew that Guillaume was right and I was wrong, that I had done something awful. And he went to the cash-register and took out some money – but I knew that he knew that there was not much money *in* the cash-register at such an hour – and pushed it at me and said, 'Take it! Take it! Better to give it to you than have you steal it from me at night! Now go!' And, oh, the faces in that bar, you should have seen them, they were so wise and tragic and they knew that *now* they knew everything, that they had always known it, and they were so glad that they had never had anything to do with me. Ah! *Les encules!* The dirty sons-of-bitches! *Les gonzesses!'* He was weeping again, with rage this time. 'Then, at last, I struck him and then many hands grabbed me and now I hardly know what happened but by and by I was in the street, with all these torn bills in my hand and everybody staring at me. I did not know what to do, I hated to walk away but I knew if anything more happened the police would come and Guillaume would have me put in jail. But I will see him again, I swear it, and on that day – !'

He stopped and sat down, staring at the wall. Then he turned to me. He watched me for a long time, in silence. Then, 'If you were not here,' he said, very slowly, 'this would be the end of Giovanni.'

I stood up. 'Don't be silly,' I said. 'It's not so tragic as all that.' I paused. 'Guillaume's disgusting. They all are. But it's not the worst thing that ever happened to you. Is it?'

'Maybe everything bad that happens to you makes you weaker,' said Giovanni, as though he had not heard me, 'and so you can stand less and less.' Then, looking up at me, 'No. The worst thing happened to me long ago and my life has been awful since that day. You are not going to leave me, are you?'

I laughed, 'Of course not.' I started shaking the broken glass off our blanket onto the floor.

'I do not know what I would do if you left me.' For the first time I felt the suggestion of a threat in his voice – or I put it there. 'I have been alone so long – I do not think I would be able to live if I had to be alone again.'

'You aren't alone now,' I said. And then, quickly, for I could not, at that moment, have endured his touch: 'Shall we go for a walk? Come – out of this room for a minute.' I grinned and cuffed him roughly, football fashion, on the neck. Then we clung together for an instant. I pushed him away. 'I'll buy you a drink,' I said.

'And will you bring me home again?' he asked.

'Yes. I'll bring you home again.'

'*Je t'aime, tu sais?*'

'*Je le sais, mon vieux.*'

He went to the sink and started washing his face. He combed his hair. I watched him. He grinned at me in the mirror, looking, suddenly, beautiful and happy. And young – I had never in my life before felt so helpless or so old.

'But we will be alright!' he cried. '*N'est-ce pas?*'

'Certainly,' I said.

He turned from the mirror. He was serious again. 'But you know – I do not know how long it will be before I find another job. And we have almost no money. Do you have any money? Did any money come from New York for you today?'

'No money came from New York, today,' I said, calmly, 'but I have a little money in my pocket.' I took it all out and put it on the table. 'About four thousand francs.'

'And I' – he went through his pockets, scattering bills and change. He shrugged and smiled at me, that fantastically sweet and helpless and moving smile. '*Je m'excuse.* I went a little mad.' He went down on his hands and knees and gathered it up and put it on the table beside the money I had placed there. About three thousand francs' worth of bills had to be pasted together and we put those aside until later. The rest of the money on the table totalled about nine thousand francs.

'We are not rich,' said Giovanni, grimly, 'but we will eat tomorrow.'

I somehow did not want him to be worried. I could not endure that look on his face. 'I'll write my father again tomorrow,' I said. 'I'll tell him some kind of lie, some kind of lie that he'll believe and I'll *make* him send me some money.' And I moved toward him as though I were driven, putting my hands on his shoulders, and forcing myself to look into his eyes. I smiled and I really felt at that moment that Judas and the Saviour had met in me. 'Don't be frightened. Don't worry.'

And I also felt, standing so close to him, feeling such a passion to keep him from terror, that a decision – once again! – had been taken from my hands. For neither my father, nor Hella, was real at that moment. And yet even this was not as real as my despairing sense that nothing was real for me, nothing would ever be real for me again – unless, indeed, this sensation of falling was reality.

The hours of this night begin to dwindle and now, with every second that passes on the clock, the blood at the bottom of my heart begins to boil, to bubble, and I know that no matter what I do anguish is about to overtake me in this house, as naked and silver as that great knife which Giovanni will be facing very soon. My executioners are here with me, walking up and down with me, washing things, and packing, and drinking from my bottle. They are everywhere I turn. Walls, windows, mirrors, water, the night outside – they are everywhere. I might call – as Giovanni, at this moment, lying in his cell, might call. But no one will hear. I might try to explain. Giovanni tried to explain. I might ask to be forgiven – if I could name and face my crime, if there were anything, or anybody, anywhere, with the power to forgive.

No. It would help if I were able to feel guilty. But the end of innocence is also the end of guilt.

No matter how it seems now, I must confess: I loved him. I do not think that I will ever love anyone like that again. And this

99

might be a great relief if I did not also know that, when the knife has fallen, Giovanni, if he feels anything will feel relief.

I walk up and down this house – up and down this house. I think of prison. Long ago, before I had ever met Giovanni, I met a man at a party at Jacques' house who was celebrated because he had spent half his life in prison. He had then written a book about it which displeased the prison authorities and won a literary prize. But this man's life was over. He was fond of saying that, since to be in prison was simply not to live, the death penalty was the only merciful verdict any jury could deliver. I remember thinking that, in effect, he had never left prison, prison was all that was real to him, he could speak of nothing else. All his movements, even to the lighting of a cigarette, were stealthy, wherever his eyes focussed one saw wall rise up. His face, the color of his face, brought to mind darkness and dampness, I felt that if one cut him his flesh would be the flesh of mushrooms. And he described to us, in avid, nostalgic detail, the barred windows, the barred doors, the judas, the guards standing at far ends of corridors, under the light. It is three tiers high inside the prison and everything is the color of gunmetal. Everything is dark and cold, except for those patches of light, where authority stands. There is on the air, perpetually, the memory of fists against the metal, a dull, booming tom-tom possibility, like the possibility of madness. The guards move and mutter and pace the corridors and boom dully up and down the stairs. They are in black, they carry guns, they are always afraid, they scarcely dare be kind. Three tiers down, in the prison's center, is the prison's great, cold heart, there is always activity: trusted prisoners wheeling things about, going in and out of the offices, ingratiating themselves with the guards for privileges of cigarettes, alcohol, and sex. The night deepens in the prison, there is muttering everywhere, and everybody knows – somehow – that death will be entering the prison courtyard early in the morning. Very early in the morning, before the trusties begin wheeling great garbage cans of food along the corridors, three men in black will come noiselessly down the corridor, one of them will turn the key in the lock. They will lay hands on someone and rush him down the corridor, first to the priest and then to a door which will open only for him, which will allow him, perhaps, one glimpse of the morning before he is thrown forward on his belly on a board and the knife falls on his neck.

I wonder about the size of Giovanni's cell. I wonder if it is bigger than his room. I know that it is colder. I wonder if he is alone or with two or three others; if he is perhaps playing cards, or smoking, or talking, or writing a letter – to whom would he be writing a letter? – or walking up and down. I wonder if he knows that the approaching morning is the last morning of his life. (For the prisoner, usually, does not know: the lawyer knows and tells the family or friends but does not tell the prisoner.) I wonder if he cares. Whether he knows or not, cares or not, he is certainly afraid. Whether he is with others or not, he is certainly alone. I try to see him, his back to me, standing at the window of his cell. From where he is perhaps he can only see the opposite wing of the prison; perhaps, by straining a little, just over the high wall, a patch of the street outside. I do not know if his hair has been cut or is long – I should think it would have been cut. I wonder if he is shaven. And now a million details, proof and fruit of intimacy, flood my mind. I wonder, for example, if he feels the need to go to the bathroom, if he has been able to eat today, if he is sweating, or dry. I wonder if anyone has made love to him in prison. And then something shakes me, I feel shaken hard and dry, like some dead thing in the desert, and I know that I am hoping that Giovanni is being sheltered in someone's arms tonight. I wish that someone were here with me. I would make love to whoever was here all night long, I would labor with Giovanni all night long.

Those days after Giovanni had lost his job, we dawdled; dawdled as doomed mountain climbers may be said to dawdle above the chasm, held only by a snapping rope. I did not write my father – I put it off from day to day. It would have been too definitive an act. I knew which lie I would tell him and I knew the lie would work – only – I was not sure that it would be a lie. Day after day we lingered in that room and Giovanni began to work on it again. He had some weird idea that it would be nice to have a bookcase sunk in the wall and he chipped through the wall until he came to the brick and began pounding away at the brick. It was hard work, it was insane work, but I did not have the energy or the heart to stop him. In a way he was doing it for me, to prove his love for me. He wanted me to stay in the room with him. Perhaps he was trying, with his own strength, to push back the encroaching walls, without, however, having the walls fall down.

Now – now, of course, I see something very beautiful in those days, which were such torture then. I felt, then, that Giovanni was dragging me with him to the bottom of the sea. He could not find a job. I knew that he was not really looking for one, that he could not. He had been bruised, so to speak, so badly that the eyes of strangers lacerated him like salt. He could not endure being very far from me for very long. I was the only person on God's cold, green earth who cared about him, who knew his speech and silence, knew his arms, and did not carry a knife. The burden of his salvation seemed to be on me and I could not endure it.

And the money dwindled – it went, it did not dwindle, very fast. Giovanni tried to keep panic out of his voice when he asked me, each morning, 'Are you going to American Express today?'

'Certainly,' I would answer.

'Do you think your money will be there today?'

'I don't know.'

'What are they *doing* with your money in New York?'

Still, still, I could not act. I went to Jacques and borrowed ten thousand francs from him again. I told him that Giovanni and I were going through a difficult time but that it would be over soon.

'He was very nice about it,' said Giovanni.

'He *can*, sometimes, be a very nice man.' We were sitting on a terrace near Odéon. I looked at Giovanni and thought, for a moment, how nice it would be if Jacques would take him off my hands.

'What are you thinking?' asked Giovanni.

For a moment I was frightened and I was also ashamed. 'I was thinking,' I said, 'that I'd like to get out of Paris.'

'Where would you like to go?' he asked.

'Oh, I don't know. Anywhere. I'm sick of this city,' I said suddenly, with a violence that surprised us both. 'I'm tired of this ancient pile of stone and all these goddam, smug people. Everything you put your hands on here comes to pieces in your hands.'

'That,' said Giovanni, gravely, 'is true.' He was watching me with a terrible intensity. I forced myself to look at him and smile.

'Wouldn't you like to get out of here for awhile?' I asked.

'Ah!' he said, and raised both hands, briefly, palms outward, in a kind of mock resignation. 'I would like to go wherever you go. I do not feel so strongly about Paris as you do, suddenly. I have never liked Paris very much.'

'Perhaps,' I said – I scarcely knew what I was saying – 'we could go to the country. Or to Spain.'

'Ah,' he said, lightly, 'you are lonely for your mistress.'

I was guilty and irritated and full of love and pain. I wanted to kick him and I wanted to take him in my arms. 'That's no reason to go to Spain,' I said, sullenly. 'I'd just like to see it, that's all. This city is expensive.'

'Well,' he said, brightly, 'let us go to Spain, perhaps it will remind me of Italy.'

'Would you rather go to Italy? Would you rather visit your home?'

He smiled. 'I do not think I have a home there any more.'

And then: 'No. I would not like to go to Italy – perhaps after all, for the same reason you do not want to go to the United States.'

'But I *am* going to the United States,' I said, quickly. And he looked at me. 'I mean, I'm certainly going to go back there one of these days.'

'One of these days,' he said. 'Everything bad will happen – one of these days.'

'Why is it bad?'

He smiled, 'Why, you will go home and then you will find that home is not home any more. Then you will really be in trouble. As long as you stay here, you can always think: One day I will go home.' He played with my thumb and grinned. '*N'est-ce pas?*'

'Beautiful logic,' I said. 'You mean I have a home to go to as long as I don't go there?'

He laughed. 'Well, isn't it true? You don't have a home until you leave it and then, when you have left it, you never can go back.'

'I seem,' I said, 'to have heard this song before.'

'Ah, *yes*,' said Giovanni, 'and you will certainly hear it again. It is one of those songs that somebody, somewhere, will always be singing.'

We rose and started walking. 'And what would happen,' I asked, idly, 'if I shut my ears?'

He was silent for a long while. Then: 'You do, sometimes, remind me of the kind of man who is tempted to put himself in prison in order to avoid being hit by a car.'

'That,' I said, sharply, 'would seem to apply much more to you than to me.'

'What do you mean?' he asked.

'I'm talking about that room, that hideous room. Why have you buried yourself there so long?'

'Buried myself? Forgive me, *mon cher Americain*, but Paris is not like New York, it is not full of palaces for boys like me. Do you think I should be living in Versailles instead?'

'There must – there must,' I said, 'be other rooms.'

'*Ca ne manque, les chambres.* The world is full of rooms – big rooms, little rooms, round rooms, square ones, rooms high up, rooms low down – all kinds of rooms! What kind of room do you think Giovanni should be living in? How long do you think it took me to find the room I have? And since when, since when' – he stopped and beat with his forefinger on my chest – 'have you so hated the room? Since when? Since yesterday, since always? *Dis-moi.*'

Facing him, I faltered. 'I don't hate it. I – I didn't mean to hurt your feelings.'

His hands dropped to his sides. His eyes grew big. He laughed. 'Hurt my *feelings*! Am I now a stranger that you speak to me like that, with such an American politeness?'

'All I mean, baby, is that I wish we could move.'

'We can move. Tomorrow! Let us go to a hotel. Is that what you want? *Le Crillon peut-être?*'

I sighed, speechless, and we started walking again.

'I know,' he burst out, after a moment, 'I know! You want to leave Paris, you want to leave the room – ah! you are wicked. *Comme tu es mérchant!*'

'You misunderstand me,' I said. 'You misunderstand me.'

He smiled grimly, to himself. *'J'espère bien.'*

Later, when we were back in the room, putting the loose bricks Giovanni had taken out of the wall into a sack, he asked me, 'This girl of yours – have you heard from her lately?'

'Not lately,' I said. I did not look up. 'But I expect her to turn up in Paris almost any day now.'

He stood up, standing in the center of the room, under the light, looking at me. I stood up, too, half smiling, but also, in some strange, dim way, a little frightened.

'Viens m'embrasser,' he said.

I was vividly aware that he held a brick in his hand, I held a brick in mine. It really seemed for an instant that if I did not go to him, we would use these bricks to beat each other to death.

Yet, I could not move at once. We stared at each other across a narrow space that was full of danger, that almost seemed to roar, like a flame.

'Come,' he said.

I dropped my brick and went to him. In a moment I heard his fall. And at moments like this I felt that we were merely enduring and committing the longer and lesser and more perpetual murder.

4

At last there came the note which I had been waiting for, from Hella, telling me the day and hour she would arrive in Paris. I did not tell this to Giovanni, but walked out alone that day and went to the station to meet her.

I had hoped that when I saw her something instantaneous, definitive, would have happened to me, something to make me know where I should be and where I was. But nothing happened. I recognized her at once, before she saw me, she was wearing green, her hair was a little shorter, and her face was tan, and she wore the same brilliant smile. I loved her as much as ever and I still did not know how much that was.

When she saw me she stood stock-still on the platform, her hands clasped in front of her, with her wide-legged, boyish stance, smiling. For a moment we simply stared at each other.

'*Eh bien*,' she said, '*t'embrasse pas ta femme?*'

Then I took her in my arms and something happened then. I was terribly glad to see her. It really seemed, with Hella in the circle of my arms, that my arms were home and I was welcoming her back there. She fitted in my arms, she always had, and the shock of holding her caused me to feel that my arms had been empty since she had been away.

I held her very close in that high, dark shed, with a great confusion of people all about us, just beside the breathing train. She smelled of the wind and the sea and of space and I felt in her marvellously living body the possibility of legitimate surrender.

Then she pulled away. Her eyes were damp. 'Let me look at you,' she said. She held me at arm's length, searching my face. 'Ah. You look wonderful. I'm so happy to see you again.'

I kissed her lightly on the nose and felt that I had passed the first inspection. I picked up her bags and we started toward the exit. 'Did you have a good trip? And how was Seville? And how do you like bull-fights? Did you meet any bull-fighters? Tell me everything.'

She laughed. 'Everything is a very tall order. I had a terrible trip, I hate trains, I wish I'd flown but I've been in one Spanish airplane and I swore never, never again. It rattled, my dear, in the middle of the air just like a model T Ford – it had probably *been* a model T Ford at one time – and I just sat there, praying and drinking brandy. I was sure I'd never see land again.' We passed through the barrier, into the streets. Hella looked about delightedly at all of it, the cafés, the self-contained people, the violent snarl of the traffic, the blue-caped traffic policeman and his white, gleaming club. 'Coming back to Paris,' she said, after a moment, 'is always so lovely, no matter where you've been.' We got into a cab and our driver made a wide, reckless circle into the stream of traffic. 'I should think that even if you returned here in some awful sorrow, you might – well, you might find it possible here to begin to be reconciled.'

'Let's hope,' I said, 'that we never have to put Paris to that test.'

Her smile was at once bright and melancholy. 'Let's hope.' Then she suddenly took my face between her hands and kissed me. There was a great question in her eyes and I knew that she burned to have this question answered at once. But I could not do it yet. I held her close and kissed her, closing my eyes. Everything was as it had been between us and at the same time everything was different.

I told myself I would not think about Giovanni yet, I would not worry about him yet; for tonight, anyway, Hella and I should be together with nothing to divide us. Still, I knew very well that this was not really possible: he had already divided us. I tried not to think of him sitting alone in that room, wondering why I stayed away so long.

Then we were sitting together in Hella's room on the rue de Tournon, sampling Fundador. 'It's much too sweet,' I said. 'Is this what they drink in Spain?'

'I never saw any Spaniards drinking it,' she said, and laughed.

'*They* drink wine. *I* drank gin-fizz – in Spain I somehow had the feeling that it was healthy,' and she laughed again.

I kept kissing her and holding her, trying to find my way in her again, as though she were a familiar, darkened room in which I fumbled to find the light. And, with my kisses, I was trying also to delay the moment which would commit me to her, or fail to commit me to her. But I think she felt that the indefinitive constraint between us was of her doing and all on her side. She was remembering that I had written her less and less often while she had been away. In Spain, until near the end, this had probably not worried her; not until she herself had come to a decision did she begin to be afraid that I might also have arrived at a decision, opposite to hers. Perhaps she had kept me dangling too long.

She was by nature forthright and impatient; she suffered when things were not clear; yet she forced herself to wait for some word or sign from me and held the reins of her strong desire tightly in her hands.

I wanted to force her to relinquish the reins. Somehow, I would be tongue-tied until I took her again. I hoped to burn out, through Hella, my image of Giovanni and the reality of his touch – I hoped to drive out fire with fire. Yet, my sense of what I was doing made me double-minded. And at last she asked me, with a smile, 'Have I been away too long?'

'I don't know,' I said. 'It's been a long time.'

'It was a very lonely time,' she said, unexpectedly. She turned slightly away from me, lying on her side, looking toward the window. 'I felt so aimless – like a tennis ball, bouncing, bouncing – I began to wonder where I'd land. I began to feel that I'd, somewhere, missed the boat.' She looked at me. 'You know the boat I'm talking about. They make movies about it where I come from. It's the boat that, when you miss it, it's a boat, but when it comes in, it's a ship.' I watched her face. It was stiller than I had ever known it to be before.

'Didn't you like Spain,' I asked, nervously, 'at all?'

She ran one hand, impatiently, through her hair. 'Oh. Of course, I like Spain, why not? It's very beautiful. I just didn't know what I was doing there. And I'm beginning to be tired of being in places for no particular reason.'

I lit a cigarette and smiled. 'But you went to Spain to get away from me – remember?'

She smiled and stroked my cheek. 'I haven't been very nice to you, have I?'

'You've been very honest.' I stood up and walked a little away from her. 'Did you get much thinking done, Hella?'

'I told you in my letter – don't *you* remember?'

For a moment everything seemed perfectly still. Even the faint street noises died. I had my back to her but I felt her eyes. I felt her waiting – everything seemed to be waiting.

'I wasn't sure about that letter.' I was thinking, *Perhaps I can get out of it without having to tell her anything*. 'You were sort of – offhand – I couldn't be sure whether you were glad or sorry to be throwing in with me.'

'Oh,' she said, 'but we've always been offhand, it's the only way I could have said it. I was afraid of embarrassing you – don't you understand that?'

What I wanted to suggest was that she was taking me out of desperation, less because she wanted me than because I was there. But I could not say it. I sensed that, though it might be true, she no longer knew it.

'But perhaps,' she said, carefully, 'you feel differently now. Please say so if you do.' She waited for my answer for a moment. Then: 'You know, I'm not really the emancipated girl I try to be at all. I guess I just want a man to come home to me every night. I want to be able to sleep with a man without being afraid he's going to knock me up. Hell, I want to be knocked up. I want to start having babies. In a way, it's really all I'm good for.' There was silence again. 'Is that what you want?'

'Yes,' I said, 'I've always wanted that.'

I turned to face her, very quickly, or as though strong hands on my shoulders had turned me around. The room was darkening. She lay on the bed, watching me, her mouth slightly open, and her eyes like lights. I was terribly aware of her body, and of mine.

I walked over to her and put my head on her breast. I wanted to lie there, hidden and still. But then, deep within, I felt her moving, rushing to open the gates of her strong, walled city and let the king of glory come in.

Dear Dad, I wrote, *I won't keep any secrets from you any more, I found a girl and I want to marry her and it wasn't that I was keeping secrets from you, I just wasn't sure she wanted to marry me. But she's finally agreed to risk it, poor soft-headed thing that she is, and we're planning to tie the knot while we're still over here and make our way home by easy stages. She's not French, in case you're worried (I know you don't dislike the French, it's just that you don't think they have our virtues – I might add, they don't). Anyway, Hella – her name is Hella Lincoln, she comes from Minneapolis, her father and mother still live there, he's a corporation lawyer, she's just the little woman – Hella would like us to honeymoon here and it goes without saying that I like anything she likes. So. Now will you send your loving son some of his hard-earned money. Tout de suite. That's French for pronto.*

Hella – the photo doesn't really do her justice – came over here a couple of years ago to study painting. Then she discovered she wasn't a painter and just about the time she was ready to throw herself into the Seine, we met, and the rest, as they say, is history. I know you'll love her, Dad, and she'll love you. She's already made me a very happy man.

Hella and Giovanni met by accident, after Hella had been in Paris for three days. During those three days I had not seen him and I had not mentioned his name.

We had been wandering about the city all day and all day Hella had been full of a subject which I had never heard her discuss at such length before: women. She claimed it was hard to be one.

'I don't see what's so hard about being a woman. At least, not as long as she's got a man.'

'That's just it,' said she. 'Hasn't it ever struck you that that's a sort of humiliating necessity?'

'Oh, please,' I said. 'It never seemed to humiliate any of the women I knew.'

'Well,' she said, 'I'm sure you never thought about any of them – in that way.'

'I certainly didn't. I hope they didn't, either. And why are *you*? What's *your* beef?'

'I've got no *beef*,' she said. She hummed, low in her throat, a kind of playful, Mozart tune. 'I've got no beef at all. But it does seem – well, difficult – to be at the mercy of some gross, unshaven stranger before you can begin to be yourself.'

'I don't know if I like *that*,' I said. 'Since when have I been gross? or a stranger? It may be true that I need a shave but that's *your* fault, I haven't been able to tear myself away from you.' And I grinned and kissed her.

'Well,' she said, 'you may not be a stranger *now*. But you were once and I'm sure you will be again – many times.'

'If it comes to that,' I said, 'so will you be, for me.'

She looked at me with a quick, bright smile. 'Will I?' Then: 'But what I mean about being a woman is, we might get married now and stay married for fifty years and I might be a stranger to you every instant of that time and you might never know it.'

'But if *I* were a stranger – *you* would know it?'

'For a woman,' she said, 'I think a man is always a stranger. And there's something awful about being at the mercy of a stranger.'

'But men are at the mercy of women, too. Have you never thought of that?'

'Ah!' she said, 'men may be at the mercy of women – I think men like that idea, it strokes the misogynist in them. But if a particular *man* is ever at the mercy of a particular *woman* – why, he's somehow stopped being a man. And the lady, then, is more neatly trapped than ever.'

'You mean, I can't be at your mercy? But you can be at mine?' I laughed. 'I'd like to see you at *anybody's* mercy, Hella.'

'You may laugh,' she said, humorously, 'but there is something in what I say. I began to realize it in Spain – that I wasn't free, that I couldn't be free until I was attached – no, *committed* – to someone.'

'To someone? Not some*thing?*'

She was silent. 'I don't know,' she said at last, 'but I'm beginning to think that women get attached to some*thing* really by default. They'd give it up, if they could, anytime, for a man. Of course they can't admit this, and neither can most of them let go of what they have. But I think it kills them – perhaps I only mean,' she added, after a moment, 'that it would have killed *me.*'

'What do you want, Hella? What have you got now that makes such a difference?'

She laughed. 'It isn't what I've *got.* It isn't even what I *want.* It's that *you've* got *me.* So now I can be – your obedient and most loving servant.'

I felt cold. I shook my head in mock confusion. 'I don't know what you're talking about.'

'Why,' she said, 'I'm talking about my life. I've got you to take care of and feed and torment and trick and love – I've got you to put up with. From now on, I can have a wonderful time com-plaining about being a woman. But I won't be terrified that I'm *not* one.' She looked at my face, and laughed. 'Oh, I'll be doing other *things,*' she cried. 'I won't stop being intelligent. I'll read and argue and *think* and all that – and I'll make a great point of not thinking *your* thoughts – and you'll be pleased because I'm sure the resulting confusion will cause you to see that I've only got a finite woman's mind, after all. And, if God is good, you'll love me more and more and we'll be quite happy.' She laughed again. 'Don't bother your head about it, sweetheart. Leave it to me.'

Her amusement was contagious and I shook my head again, laughing with her. 'You're adorable,' I said. 'I don't understand you at all.'

She laughed again. 'There,' she said, 'that's fine. We're both taking to it like ducks to water.'

We were passing a book-store and she stopped. 'Can we go in for just a minute?' she asked. 'There's a book I'd like to get. Quite,' she added, as we entered the shop, 'a trivial book.'

I watched her with amusement as she went over to speak to the woman who ran the shop. I wandered idly over to the farthest book shelf, where a man stood, his back to me, leafing through a magazine. As I stood beside him, he closed the magazine and put it down, and turned. We recognized each other at once. It was Jacques.

'*Tiens!*' he cried. 'Here you are! We were beginning to think that you had gone back to America.'

'Me?' I laughed. 'No, I'm still in Paris. I've just been busy.' Then, with a terrible suspicion, I asked, 'Who's *we?*'

'Why,' said Jacques, with a hard, insistent smile, 'your baby. It seems you left him alone in that room without any food, without any money, without, even, any cigarettes. He finally persuaded his concierge to allow him to put a phone call on his bill and called me. The poor boy sounded as though he would have put his head in the gas oven. If,' he laughed, 'he had *had* a gas oven.'

We stared at each other. He, deliberately, said nothing. I did not know what to say.

'I threw a few provisions in my car,' said Jacques, 'and hurried out to get him. He thought we should drag the river for you. But I assured him that he did not know Americans as well as I and that you had not drowned yourself. You had only disappeared in order – to think. And I see that I was right. You have thought so much that now you must find what others have thought before you. One book,' he said, finally, 'that you can surely spare yourself the trouble of reading is the Marquis de Sade.'

'Where is Giovanni now?' I asked.

'I finally remembered the name of Hella's hotel,' said Jacques. 'Giovanni said that you were more or less expecting her and so I gave him the bright idea of calling you there. He has stepped out for an instant to do just that. He'll be along presently.'

Hella had returned, with her book.

'You two have met before,' I said, awkwardly. 'Hella, you remember Jacques.'

She remembered him and also remembered that she disliked him. She smiled politely and held out her hand. 'How are you?'

'*Je suis ravi, mademoiselle,*' said Jacques. He knew that Hella disliked him and this amused him. And, to corroborate her dislike, and also because at that moment he really hated me, he bowed low over her outstretched hand and became, in an instant, outrageously and offensively effeminate. I watched him as though I were watching an imminent disaster from many miles away. He turned playfully to me. 'David has been hiding from us,' he murmured, 'now that you are back.'

'Oh?' said Hella, and moved closer to me, taking my hand, 'that was very naughty of him. I'd never have allowed it – if I'd known we were hiding.' She grinned. 'But then, he never tells me anything.'

Jacques looked at her. 'No doubt,' he said, 'he finds more fascinating topics when you are together than why he hides from old friends.'

I felt a great need to get out of there before Giovanni arrived. 'We haven't eaten supper yet,' I said, trying to smile, 'perhaps we can meet you later?' I knew that my smile was begging him to be kind to me.

But at that moment the tiny bell which announced every entry into the shop rang, and Jacques said, 'Ah. Here is Giovanni.' And, indeed, I felt him behind me, standing stock-still, staring, and felt in Hella's clasp, in her entire body, a kind of wild shrinking and not all of her composure kept this from showing in her face. When Giovanni spoke his voice was thick with fury and relief and unshed tears.

'Where have you been?' he cried. 'I thought you were dead! I thought you had been knocked down by a car or thrown into the river – what have you been doing all these days?'

I was able, oddly enough, to smile. And I was astonished at my calm. 'Giovanni,' I said, 'I want you to meet my fiancée. Mlle Hella. Monsieur Giovanni.'

He had seen her before his outburst ended and now he touched her hand with a still, astounded politeness and stared at her with black, steady eyes as though he had never seen a woman before.

'*Enchanté, mademoiselle,*' he said. And his voice was dead and cold. He looked briefly at me, then back at Hella. For a moment we, all four, stood there as though we were posing for a tableau.

'Really,' said Jacques, 'now that we are all together, I think we should have one drink together. A very short one,' he said to Hella, cutting off her attempt at polite refusal, and taking her arm. 'It's not every day,' he said, 'that old friends get together.' He forced us to move, Hella and he together, Giovanni and I ahead. The bell rang viciously as Giovanni opened the door. The evening air hit us like a blaze. We started walking away from the river, toward the boulevard.

'When I decide to leave a place,' said Giovanni, 'I tell the concierge, so that at least she will know where to forward my mail.'

I flared briefly, unhappily. I had noticed that he was shaven and wore a clean, white shirt and tie – a tie which surely belonged to Jacques. 'I don't see what you've got to complain about,' I said. 'You sure knew where to go.'

But with the look he gave me then my anger left me and I wanted to cry. 'You are not nice,' he said. '*Tu n'est pas chic du tout.*' Then he said no more and we walked to the boulevard in silence. Behind us I could hear the murmur of Jacques' voice. On the corner we stood and waited for them to catch up with us.

'Darling,' said Hella, as she reached me, 'you stay and have a drink if you want to. I can't, I really can't, I don't feel well at all.' She turned to Giovanni. 'Please forgive me,' she said, 'but I've just come back from Spain and I've hardly sat down a moment since I got off the train. Another time, truly – but I *must* get some sleep tonight.' She smiled and held out her hand but he did not seem to see it.

'I'll walk Hella home,' I said, 'and then I'll come back. If you'll tell me where you're going to be.'

Giovanni laughed, abruptly. 'Why, we will be in the quarter,' he said. 'We will not be difficult to find.'

'I am sorry,' said Jacques, to Hella, 'that you do not feel well. Perhaps another time.' And Hella's hand, which was still uncertainly outstretched, he bowed over and kissed a second time. He straightened and looked at me. 'You must bring Hella to dinner at my house one night.' He made a face. 'There is no need to hide your fiancée from us.'

'No need whatever,' said Giovanni. 'She is very charming. And we' – with a grin, to Hella – 'will try to be charming, too.'

'Well,' I said, and took Hella by the arm, 'I'll see you later.'

'If I am not here,' said Giovanni, both vindictive and near tears, 'by the time you come back again, I will be at home. You remember where that is – ? It is near a zoo.'

'I remember,' I said. I started backing away, as though I were backing out of a cage, 'I'll see you later. *A tout à l'heure.*'

'*A la prochaine,*' said Giovanni.

I felt their eyes on our backs as we walked away from them. For a long while Hella was silent – possibly because, like me, she was afraid to say anything. Then: 'I really can't stand that man. He gives me the creeps.' After a moment: 'I didn't know you'd seen so much of him while I was away.'

'I didn't,' I said. To do something with my hands, to give myself a moment of privacy, I stopped and lit a cigarette. I felt her eyes. But she was not suspicious; she was only troubled.

'And who is Giovanni?' she asked, when we started walking again. She gave a little laugh. 'I just realized that I haven't even asked you where you were living. Are you living with him?'

'We've been sharing a maid's room out at the end of Paris,' I said.

'Then it wasn't very nice of you,' said Hella, 'to go off for so long, without any warning.'

'Well, my God,' I said, 'he's only my room-mate. How was I to know he'd start dragging the river just because I stayed out a couple of nights?'

'Jacques said you left him there without any money, without any cigarettes, or anything, and you didn't even tell him you were going to be with me.'

'There are lots of things I didn't tell Giovanni. But he's never made any kind of scene before – I guess he must be drunk. I'll talk to him later.'

'Are you going to go back there later?'

'Well,' I said, 'if I don't go back there later, I'll go on over to the room. I've been meaning to do that, anyway.' I grinned. 'I have to get shaved.'

Hella sighed. 'I didn't mean to get your friends mad at you,' she said. 'You ought to go back and have a drink with them. You said you were going to.'

'Well, I may, I may not. I'm not married to them, you know.'

'Well, the fact that you're going to be married to *me* doesn't mean you have to break your word to your friends. It doesn't even mean,' she added, shortly, 'that I have to *like* your friends.'

'Hella,' I said, 'I am perfectly aware of that.'

We turned off the boulevard, toward her hotel.

'He's very intense, isn't he?' she said. I was staring at the dark mound of the Senate, which ended our dark, slightly uphill street.

'Who is?'

'Giovanni. He's certainly very fond of you.'

'He's Italian,' I said. 'Italians are theatrical.'

'Well, this one,' she laughed, 'must be special, even in Italy! How long have you been living with him?'

'A couple of months.' I threw away my cigarette, 'I ran out of money while you were away – you know, I'm still waiting for money – and I moved in with him because it was cheaper. At that time he had a job and was living with his mistress most of the time.'

'Oh?' she said. 'He has a mistress?'

'He had a mistress,' I said. 'He also had a job. He's lost both.'

'Poor boy,' she said. 'No wonder he looks so lost.'

'He'll be alright,' I said, briefly. We were before her door. She pressed the night-bell.

'Is he a very good friend of Jacques?' she asked.

'Perhaps,' I said, 'not quite good enough to please Jacques.'

She laughed. 'I always feel a cold wind go over me,' she said, 'when I find myself in the presence of a man who dislikes women as much as Jacques does.'

'Well, then,' I said, 'we'll just keep him away from you. We don't want no cold winds blowing over this girl.' I kissed her on the tip of her nose. At the same moment there was a rumble from deep within the hotel and the door unlocked itself with a small, violent shudder. Hella looked humorously into the blackness. 'I always wonder,' she said, 'if I *dare* go in.' Then she looked up at me. 'Well?

Do you want to have a drink upstairs before you go back to join your friends?'

'Sure,' I said. We tiptoed into the hotel, closing the door gently behind us. My fingers finally found the *minuterie* and the weak, yellow light spilled over us. A voice, completely unintelligible, shouted out at us and Hella shouted back her name, which she tried to pronounce with a French accent. As we started up the stairs, the light went out and Hella and I began to giggle like two children. We were unable to find the minute-switch on any of the landings – I don't know why we both found this so hilarious, but we did, and we held on to each other, giggling, all the way to Hella's top-floor room.

'Tell me about Giovanni,' she asked, much later, while we lay in bed and watched the black night tease her stiff, white curtains. 'He interests me.'

'That's a pretty tactless thing to say at this moment,' I told her. 'What the hell do you mean, he interests you?'

'I mean who he is, what he thinks about. How he got that face.'

'What's the matter with his face?'

'Nothing. He's very beautiful, as a matter of fact. But there's something in that face – so old-fashioned.'

'Go to sleep,' I said. 'You're babbling.'

'How did you meet him?'

'Oh. In a bar one drunken night, with lots of other people.'

'Was Jacques there?'

'I don't remember. Yes, I guess so. I guess he met Giovanni at the same time I did.'

'What made you go to live with him?'

'I told you. I was broke and he had this room –'

'But that can't have been the *only* reason.'

'Oh, well,' I said, 'I liked him.'

'And don't you like him any more?'

'I'm very fond of Giovanni. You didn't see him at his best tonight, but he's a very nice man.' I laughed; covered by the night, emboldened by Hella's body and my own, and protected by the tone of my voice, I found great relief in adding: 'I love him, in a way. I really do.'

'He seems to feel that you have a funny way of showing it.'

'Oh, well,' I said, 'these people have another style from us. They're much more demonstrative. I can't help it. I just can't – do all that.'

'Yes,' she said, thoughtfully, 'I've noticed that.'

'You've noticed what?'

'Kids here – they think nothing of showing a lot of affection for each other. It's sort of a shock at first. Then you begin to think it's sort of nice.'

'It *is* sort of nice,' I said.

'Well,' said Hella, 'I think we ought to take Giovanni out to dinner or something one of these days. After all, he did sort of rescue you.'

'That's a good idea,' I said. 'I don't know what he's doing these days but I imagine he'll have a free evening.'

'Does he hang around with Jacques much?'

'No, I don't think so. I think he just ran into Jacques tonight.' I paused. 'I'm beginning to see,' I said, carefully, 'that kids like Giovanni are in a difficult position. This isn't, you know, the land of opportunity – there's no provision made for them. Giovanni's poor, I mean he comes from poor folks, and there isn't really much that he can do. And for what he *can* do, there's terrific competition. And, at that, very little money, not enough for them to be able to think of building any kind of future. That's why so many of them wander the streets and turn into gigolos and gangsters and God knows what.'

'It's cold,' she said, 'out here in the Old World.'

'Well, it's pretty cold out there in the New One, too,' I said. 'It's cold out here, period.'

She laughed. 'But we – we have our love to keep us warm.'

'We're not the first people who thought that as they lay in bed.' Nevertheless, we lay silent and still in each other's arms for a while. 'Hella,' I said at last.

'Yes?'

'Hella, when the money gets here, let's take it and get out of Paris.'

'Get out of Paris? Where do you want to go?'

'I don't care. Just out. I'm sick of Paris. I want to leave it for awhile. Let's go south. Maybe there'll be some sun.'

'Shall we get married in the south?'

'Hella,' I said, 'you have to believe me, I can't do anything or decide anything, I can't even see straight until we get out of this town. I don't want to get married here, I don't even want to think about getting married here. Let's just get out.'

'I didn't know you felt this way,' she said.

'I've been living in Giovanni's room for months,' I said, 'and I just can't stand it any more. I have to get out of there. Please.'

She laughed nervously and moved slightly away from me. 'Well, I really don't see why getting out of Giovanni's room means getting out of Paris.'

I sighed. 'Please, Hella. I don't feel like going into long explanations now. Maybe it's just that if I stay in Paris I'll keep running into Giovanni and . . .' I stopped.

'Why should that disturb you?'

'Well – I can't do anything to help him and I can't stand having him watch me – as though – I'm an American, Hella, he thinks I'm *rich*.' I paused and sat up, looking outward. She watched me.

'He's a very nice man, as I say, but he's very persistent – and he's got this *thing* about me, he thinks I'm God. And that room is so stinking and dirty. And soon winter'll be here and it's going to be cold . . .' I turned to her again and took her in my arms. 'Look. Let's just go. I'll explain a lot of things to you later – later – when we get out.'

There was a long silence.

'And you want to leave right away?' she said.

'Yes. As soon as that money comes, let's rent a house.'

'You're sure,' she said, 'that you don't just want to go back to the States?'

I groaned. 'No. Not yet. That isn't what I mean.'

She kissed me. 'I don't care where we go,' she said, 'as long as we're together.' Then she pushed me away. 'It's almost morning,' she said. 'We'd better get some sleep.'

I got to Giovanni's room very late the next evening. I had been walking by the river with Hella and, later, I drank too much in several bistros. The light crashed on as I came into the room and Giovanni sat up in bed, crying out in a voice of terror, *'Qui est là? Qui est là?'*

I stopped in the doorway, weaving a little in the light, and I said, 'It's me, Giovanni. Shut up.'

Giovanni stared at me and turned on his side, facing the wall, and began to cry.

I thought, *Sweet Jesus!* and I carefully closed the door. I took my cigarettes out of my jacket pocket and hung my jacket over the chair. With my cigarettes in my hand I went to the bed and leaned over Giovanni. I said, 'Baby, stop crying. Please stop crying.'

Giovanni turned and looked at me. His eyes were red and wet, but he wore a strange smile, it was composed of cruelty and shame and delight. He held out his arms and I leaned down, brushing his hair from his eyes.

'You smell of wine,' said Giovanni, then.

'I haven't been drinking wine. Is that what frightened you? Is that why you are crying?'

'No.'

'What is the matter?'

'Why have you gone away from me?'

I did not know what to say. Giovanni turned to the wall again. I had hoped, I had supposed that I would feel nothing: but I felt a tightening in a far corner of my heart, as though a finger had touched me there.

'I have never reached you,' said Giovanni. 'You have never really been here. I do not think you have ever lied to me but I know that you have never told me the truth – why? Sometimes you were here all day long and you read or you opened the window or you cooked something – and I watched you – and you never said anything –

and you looked at me with such eyes, as though you did not see me. All day, while I worked to make this room for you.'

I said nothing. I looked beyond Giovanni's head at the square windows which held back the feeble moonlight.

'What are you doing all the time? And why do you say nothing? You are evil, you know, and sometimes when you smiled at me I hated you. I wanted to strike you. I wanted to make you bleed. You smiled at me the way you smiled at everyone, you told me what you told everyone – and you tell nothing but lies. What are you always hiding? And do you think I did not know when you made love to me, you were making love to no one? *No one!* Or everyone – but not *me*, certainly. I am nothing to you, nothing, and you bring me fever but no delight.'

I moved, looking for a cigarette. They were in my hand. I lit one. In a moment, I thought, I will say something. I will say something and then I will walk out of this room forever.

'You know I cannot be alone. I have told you. What is the matter? Can we never have a life together?'

He began to cry again. I watched the hot tears roll from the corners of his eyes onto the dirty pillow.

'If you cannot love me, I will die. Before you came I wanted to die, I have told you many times. It is cruel to have made me want to live only to make my death more bloody.'

I wanted to say so many things. Yet, when I opened my mouth, I made no sound. And yet – I do not know what I felt for Giovanni. I felt nothing for Giovanni. I felt terror and pity and a rising lust.

He took my cigarette from my lips and puffed on it, sitting up in bed, his hair in his eyes again.

'I have never known anyone like you before. I was never like this before you came. Listen. In Italy I had a woman and she was very good to me. She loved me, she loved *me*, and she took care of me and she was always there when I came in from work, in from the vineyards, and there was never any trouble between us, never. I was young then and did not know the things I learned later or the terrible things you have taught me. I thought all women were like that. I thought all men were like me – I thought I was like all other men. I was not unhappy then and I was not lonely – for she was there – and I did not want to die. I wanted to stay forever in our village and work in the vineyards and drink the wine we made and make love to my girl. I have told you about my village – ? It is very old and in the south, it is on a hill. At night, when we walked by the wall, the world seemed to fall down before us, the whole, far-off, dirty world. I did not ever want to see it. Once we made love under the wall.

'Yes, I wanted to stay there forever and eat much spaghetti and drink much wine and make many babies and grow fat. You would not have liked me if I had stayed. I can see you, many years from now, coming through our village in the ugly, fat, American motor car you will surely have by then and looking at me and looking at all of us and tasting our wine and shitting on us with those empty smiles Americans wear everywhere and which you wear all the time and driving off with a great roar of the motors and a great sound of tires and telling all the other Americans you meet that they must come and see our village because it is so picturesque. And you will have no idea of the life there, dripping and bursting and beautiful and terrible, as you have no idea of my life now. But I think I would have been happier there and I would not have minded your smiles. I would have had my life. I have lain here many nights, waiting for you to come home, and thought how far away is my village and how terrible it is to be in this cold city, among people whom I hate, where it is cold and wet and never dry and hot as it was there, and where Giovanni has no one to talk to, and no one to be with, and where he has found a lover who is neither man nor woman, nothing that I can know or touch. You do not know, do you, what it is like to lie awake at night and wait for someone to come home? But I am sure you do not know. You do not know anything. You do not know any of the terrible things – that is why you smile and dance the way you do and you think that the comedy you are playing with the short-haired, moon-faced little girl is love.'

He dropped the cigarette to the floor, where it lay burning faintly. He began to cry again. I looked at the room, thinking: I cannot bear it.

'I left my village one wild, sweet day. I will never forget that day. It was the day of my death – I wish it had been the day of my death. I remember the sun was hot and scratchy on the back of my neck as I walked the road away from my village and the road went upward and I walked bent over, I remember everything, the brown dust at my feet, and the little pebbles which rushed before me, and the short trees along the road and all the flat houses and all their colors under the sun. I remember I was weeping, but not as I am weeping now, much worse, more terrible – since I am with you, I cannot even cry as I cried then. That was the first time in my life that I wanted to die. I had just buried my baby in the churchyard where my father and my father's fathers were and I had left my girl screaming in my mother's house. Yes, I had made a baby but it was born dead. It was all grey and twisted when I saw it and it made no sound – and we spanked it on the buttocks and we sprinkled it with holy water and we prayed but it never made a sound, it was dead. It was a little boy, it would have been a wonderful, strong man, perhaps even the kind of man *you* and Jacques and Guillaume and all your disgusting band of fairies spend all your days and nights looking for, and dreaming of – but it was dead, it was my baby and we had made it, my girl and I, and it was dead. When I knew that it was dead I took our crucifix off the wall and I spat on it and I threw it on the floor and my mother and my girl screamed and I went out. We buried it right away, the next day, and then I left my village and I came to this city where surely God has punished me for all my sins and for spitting on His holy Son, and where I will surely die. I do not think that I will ever see my village again.'

I stood up. My head was turning. Salt was in my mouth. The room seemed to rock, as it had the first time I had come here, so many lifetimes ago. I heard Giovanni's moan behind me. '*Chéri. Mon très cher.* Don't leave me. Please don't leave me.' I turned and held him in my arms staring above his head at the wall, at the man and woman on the wall who walked together among roses. He was sobbing, it would have been said, as though his heart would break. But I felt that it was my heart which was broken. Something had broken in me to make me so cold and so perfectly still and far away.

Still I had to speak.

'Giovanni,' I said. 'Giovanni.'

He began to be still, he was listening; I felt, unwillingly, not for the first time, the cunning of the desperate.

'Giovanni,' I said, 'you always knew that I would leave one day. You knew my fiancée was coming back to Paris.'

'You are not leaving me for her,' he said. 'You are leaving me for some other reason. You lie so much, you have come to believe all your own lies. But I, *I* have senses. You are not leaving me for a *woman*. If you were really in love with this little girl, you would not have had to be so cruel to me.'

'She's not a little girl,' I said. 'She's a woman and no matter what you think, I *do* love her . . .'

'You do not,' cried Giovanni, sitting up, 'love anyone! You never have loved anyone, I am sure you never will! You love your purity, you love your mirror – you are just like a little virgin, you walk around with your hands in front of you as though you had some precious metal, gold, silver, rubies, maybe *diamonds* down there between your legs! You will never give it to anybody, you will never let anybody *touch* it – man *or* woman. You want to be *clean*. You think you came here covered with soap and you think you will go out covered with soap – and you do not want to *stink*, not even for five minutes, in the meantime.' He grasped me by the collar, wrestling and caressing at once, fluid and iron at once: saliva spraying from his lips and his eyes full of tears, but with the bones of his face showing and the muscles leaping in his arms and neck. 'You want to leave Giovanni because he makes you stink. You want to despise Giovanni because he is not afraid of the stink of love. You want to *kill* him in the name of all your lying little moralities. And you – you are *immoral*. You are, by far, the most immoral man I have met in all my life. Look, *look* what you have done to me. Do you think you could have done this if I did not love you? Is *this* what you should do to love?'

'Giovanni, stop it! For God's sake, *stop* it! What in the world do you want me to do? I can't *help* the way I feel.'

'Do you *know* how you feel? Do you feel? *What* do you feel?'

'I feel nothing now,' I said, 'nothing. I want to get out of this room, I want to get away from you, I want to end this terrible scene.'

'You want to get away from me.' He laughed; he watched me; the look in his eyes was so bottomlessly bitter it was almost benevolent. 'At last you are beginning to be honest. And do you know *why* you want to get away from me?'

Inside me something locked. 'I – I cannot have a life with you,' I said.

'But you can have a life with Hella. With that moon-faced little girl who thinks babies come out of cabbages – or frigidaires, I am not acquainted with the mythology of your country. You can have a life with her.'

'Yes,' I said, wearily, 'I can have a life with her.' I stood up. I was shaking. 'What kind of life can we have in this room? – this filthy little room. What kind of life can two men have together, anyway? All this love you talk about – isn't it just that you want to be made to feel strong? You want to go out and be the laborer and bring home the money and you want me to stay here and wash the dishes and cook the food and clean this miserable closet of a room and kiss you when you come in through that door and lie with you at night and be your little *girl*. That's what you want. That's what you mean and that's *all* you mean when you say you love me. You say I want to kill *you*. What do you think you've been doing to me?'

'I am not trying to make you a little girl. If I wanted a little girl, I would be *with* a little girl.'

'Why aren't you? Isn't it just that you're afraid? And you take *me* because you haven't got the guts to go after a woman, which is what you *really* want?'

He was pale. 'You are the one who keeps talking about *what* I want. But I have only been talking about *who* I want.'

'But I'm a man,' I cried, 'a man! What do you think can *happen* between us?'

'You know very well,' said Giovanni, slowly, 'what can happen between us. It is for that reason you are leaving me.' He got up and walked to the window and opened it. '*Bon*,' he said. He struck his fist once against the window sill. '*If* I could make you stay, I would,' he shouted. 'If I had to beat you, chain you, starve you – *if* I could make you stay, I would.' He turned back into the room; the wind blew his hair. He shook his finger at me, grotesquely playful. 'One day, perhaps, you will wish I had.'

'It's cold,' I said. 'Close the window.'

He smiled. 'Now that you are leaving – you want the windows closed. *Bien sûr.*' He closed the window and we stood staring at each other in the center of the room. 'We will not fight any more,' he said. 'Fighting will not make you stay. In French we have what is called *une separation de corps* – not a divorce, you understand, just a separation. Well. We will separate. But I know you belong with me. I believe, I must believe – that you will come back.'

'Giovanni,' I said, 'I'll not be coming back. You know I won't be back.'

He waved his hand. 'I said we would not fight any more. The Americans have no sense of doom, none whatever. They do not recognize doom when they see it.' He produced a bottle from beneath the sink. 'Jacques left a bottle of cognac here. Let us have a little drink – for the road, as I believe you people say sometimes.'

I watched him. He carefully poured two drinks. I saw that he was shaking – with rage, or pain, or both.

He handed me my glass.

'*A la tienne*,' he said.

'*A la tienne.*'

We drank. I could not keep myself from asking: 'Giovanni. What are you going to do now?'

'Oh,' he said, 'I have friends. I will think of things to do. Tonight, for example, I shall have supper with Jacques. No doubt tomorrow night I shall also have supper with Jacques. He has become very fond of me. He thinks you are a monster.'

'Giovanni,' I said, helplessly, 'be careful. Please be careful.'

He gave me an ironical smile. 'Thank you,' he said. 'You should have given me that advice the night we met.'

That was the last time we really spoke to one another. I stayed with him until morning and then I threw my things into a bag and took them away with me, to Hella's place.

I will not forget the last time he looked at me. The morning light filled the room, reminding me of so many mornings and of the morning I had first come there. Giovanni sat on the bed, completely naked, holding a glass of cognac between his hands. His body was dead white, his face was wet and grey. I was at the door with my suitcase. With my hand on the knob, I looked at him. Then I wanted to beg him to forgive me. But this would have been too great a confession; any yielding at that moment would have locked me forever in that room with him. And in a way this was exactly what I wanted. I felt a tremor go through me, like the beginning of an earthquake, and felt, for an instant, that I was drowning in his eyes. His body, which I had come to know so well, glowed in the light and charged and thickened the air between us. Then something opened in my brain, a secret, noiseless door swung open, frightening me: it had not occurred to me until that instant that, in fleeing from his body, I confirmed and perpetuated his body's power over me. Now, as though I had been branded, his body was burned into my mind, into my dreams. And all this time he did not take his eyes from me. He seemed to find my face more transparent than a shop-window. He did not smile, he was neither grave, nor vindictive, nor sad; he was still. He was waiting, I think, for me to cross that space and take him in my arms again – waiting, as one waits at a death-bed for the miracle one dare not disbelieve, which will not happen. I had to get out of there for my face showed too much, the war in my body was dragging me down. My feet refused to carry me over to him again. The wind of my life was blowing me away.

'*Au revoir, Giovanni.*'

'*Au revoir, mon cher.*'

I turned from him, unlocked the door. The weary exhale of his breath seemed to ruffle my hair and brush my brow like the very wind of madness. I walked down the short corridor, expecting every instant to hear his voice behind me, passed through the vestibule, passed the *loge* of the still sleeping concierge, into the morning streets. And with every step I took it became more impossible for me to turn back. And my mind was empty – or it was as though my mind had become one enormous, anaesthetized wound. I thought only, *One day I'll weep for this. One of these days I'll start to cry.*

At the corner, in a faint patch of the morning sun, I looked in my wallet to count my bus tickets. In the wallet I found three hundred francs, taken from Hella, my *carte d'identité*, my address in the United States, and paper, paper, scraps of paper, cards, photographs. On each piece of paper I found addresses, telephone numbers, memos of various rendezvous made and kept – or perhaps not kept – people met and remembered, or perhaps not remembered, hopes probably not fulfilled: certainly not fulfilled, or I would not have been standing on that street corner.

I found four bus tickets in my wallet and I walked to the *arrêt*. There was a policeman standing there, his blue hood, weighted, hanging down behind, his white club gleaming. He looked at me and smiled and cried, '*Ca va?*'

'*Oui, merci.* And you?'

'*Toujours.* It's a nice day, no?'

'Yes.' But my voice trembled. 'The autumn is beginning.'

'*C'est ça.*' And he turned away, back to his contemplation of the boulevard. I smoothed my hair with my hand, feeling foolish for feeling shaken. I watched a woman pass, coming from the market, her string bag full; at the top, precariously, a litre of red wine. She was not young but she was clear-faced and bold, she had a strong, thick body and strong, thick hands. The policeman shouted something to her and she shouted back – something bawdy and good-natured. The policeman laughed; but refused to look at me again. I watched the woman continue down the street – home, I thought, to her husband, dressed in blue working clothes, dirty, and to her children. She passed the corner where the patch of sunlight fell and crossed the street. The bus came and the policeman and I, the only people waiting, got on – he stood on the platform, far from me. The policeman was not young, either, but he had a gusto which I admired. I looked out of the window and the streets rolled by. Ages ago, in another city, on another bus, I sat so at the windows, looking outward, inventing for each flying face which trapped my brief attention some life, some destiny, in which I played a part. I was looking for some whisper, or promise, of my possible salvation. But it seemed to me that morning that my ancient self had been dreaming the most dangerous dream of all.

The days that followed seemed to fly. It seemed to turn cold overnight. The tourists in their thousands disappeared, conjured away by time-tables. When one walked through the gardens, leaves fell about one's head and sighed and crashed beneath one's feet. The stone of the city, which had been luminous and changing, faded slowly, but with no hesitation, into simple grey stone again. It was apparent that the stone was hard. Daily, fishermen disappeared from the river until, one day, the river banks were clear. The bodies of young boys and girls began to be compromised by heavy underwear, by sweaters and mufflers, hoods and capes. Old men seemed older, old women slower. The colors on the river faded, the rain began, and the river began to rise. It was apparent that the sun would soon give up the tremendous struggle it cost her to get to Paris for a few hours every day.

'But it will be warm in the south,' I said.

The money had come. Hella and I were busy every day, on the track of a house in Eze, in Cagnes-sur-mer, in Vence, in Monte Carlo, in Antibes, in Grasse. We were scarcely ever seen in the quarter. We stayed in her room, we made love a lot, we went to the movies, and had long, frequently rather melancholy dinners in strange restaurants on the right bank. It is hard to say what produced this melancholy, which sometimes settled over us like the shadow of some vast, some predatory, waiting bird. I do not think that Hella was unhappy, for I had never before clung to her as I clung to her during that time. But perhaps she sensed, from time to time, that my clutch was too insistent to be trusted, certainly too insistent to last.

And from time to time, around the quarter, I ran into Giovanni. I dreaded seeing him, not only because he was almost always with Jacques, but also because, though he was often rather better dressed, he did not look well. I could not endure something at once abject and vicious which I began to see in his eyes, nor the way he giggled at Jacques' jokes, nor the mannerisms, a fairy's mannerisms, which he was beginning, sometimes, to affect. I did not want to know what his status was with Jacques; yet the day came when it was revealed to me in Jacques' spiteful and triumphant eyes. And Giovanni, during this short encounter, in the middle of the boulevard as dusk fell, with people hurrying all about us, was really amazingly giddy and girlish, and very drunk – it was as though he were forcing me to taste the cup of his humiliation. And I hated him for this.

The next time I saw him it was in the morning. He was buying a newspaper. He looked up at me insolently, into my eyes, and looked away. I watched him diminish down the boulevard. When I got home, I told Hella about it, trying to laugh.

Then I began to see him around the quarter without Jacques, with the street-boys of the quarter, whom he had once described to me as '*lamentable.*' He was no longer so well dressed, he was beginning to look like one of them. His special friend among them seemed to be the same, tall, pock-marked boy, named Yves, whom I remembered having seen briefly, playing the pinball machine, and, later, talking to Jacques on that first morning in Les Halles. One night, quite drunk myself, and wandering about the quarter alone, I ran into this boy and bought him a drink. I did not mention Giovanni but Yves volunteered the information that he was not with Jacques any more. But it seemed that he might be able to get back his old job in Guillaume's bar. It was certainly not more than a week after this that Guillaume was found dead in the private quarters above his bar, strangled with the sash of his dressing gown.

5

It was a terrific scandal, if you were in Paris at the time you certainly heard of it, and saw the pictures printed in all the newspapers, of Giovanni, just after he was captured. Editorials were written and speeches were made, and many bars of the genre of Guillaume's bar were closed. (But they did not stay closed long.) Plain-clothes policemen descended on the quarter, asking to see everyone's papers, and the bars were emptied of *tapettes*. Giovanni was no-where to be found. All of the evidence, above all, of course, his disappearance, pointed to him as the murderer. Such a scandal always threatens, before its reverberations cease, to rock the very foundations of the state. It is necessary to find an explanation, a solution, and a victim with the utmost possible speed. Most of the men picked up in connection with this crime were not picked up on suspicion of murder. They were picked up on suspicion of having what the French, with a delicacy I take to be sardonic, call *les gouts particuliers*. These 'tastes,' which do not constitute a crime in France, are nevertheless regarded with extreme disapprobation by the bulk of the populace, which also looks on its rulers and 'betters' with a stony lack of affection. When Guillaume's corpse was discovered it was not only the boys of the street who were frightened; they, in fact, were a good deal less frightened than the men who roamed the streets to buy them, whose careers, positions, aspirations, could never have survived such notoriety. Fathers of families, sons of great houses, and itching adventurers from Belleville were all desperately anxious that the case be closed, so that things might, in effect, go back to normal and the dreadful whiplash of public morality not fall on their backs. Until the case was closed they could not be certain which way to jump, whether they should cry out that they were martyrs, or remain what, at heart, of course, they were, simple citizens, bitter against outrage and anxious to see justice done and the health of the state preserved.

It was fortunate, therefore, that Giovanni was a foreigner. As though by some magnificently tacit agreement, with every day that he was at large, the press became more vituperative against him and more gentle toward Guillaume. It was remembered that there perished with Guillaume one of the oldest names in France. Sunday supplements were run on the history of his family; and his old, aristocratic mother, who did not survive the trial of his murderer, testified to the sterling qualities of her son and regretted that corruption had become so vast in France that such a crime could go so long unpunished. With this sentiment the populace was, of course, more than ready to agree. It is perhaps not as incredible as it certainly seemed to me, but Guillaume's name became fantastically entangled with French history, French honor, and French glory, and very nearly became, indeed, a symbol of French manhood.

'But listen,' I said to Hella, 'he was just a disgusting old fairy. That's *all* he was!'

'Well, how in the world do you expect the people who read newspapers to know that? *If* that's what he was, I'm sure he didn't advertise it – and he must have moved in a pretty limited circle.'

'Well – *somebody* knows it. Some of the people who write this drivel know it.'

'There doesn't seem to be much point,' she said, quietly, 'in defaming the dead.'

'But isn't there some point in telling the truth?'

'They're telling the truth. He's a member of a very important family and he's been murdered. I know what *you* mean. There's another truth they're *not* telling. But newspapers never do, that's not what they're for.'

I sighed. 'Poor, poor, poor Giovanni.'

'Do you believe he did it?'

'I don't know. It certainly *looks* as though he did it. He was there that night. People saw him go upstairs before the bar closed and they don't remember seeing him come down.'

'Was he working there that night?'

'Apparently not. He was just drinking. He and Guillaume seemed to have become friendly again.'

'You certainly made some peculiar friends while I was away.'

'They wouldn't seem so damn peculiar if one of them hadn't got murdered. Anyway, none of them were my friends – except Giovanni.'

'You lived with him. Can't you tell whether he'd commit murder or not?'

'How? You live with me. Can I commit a murder?'

'You? Of course not.'

'How do you *know* that? You don't know that. How do you know I'm what you see?'

'Because' – she leaned over and kissed me – 'I love you.'

'Ah! I loved Giovanni–'

'Not as I love you,' said Hella.

'I might have committed murder already, for all you know. How do you know?'

'Why are you so upset?'

'Wouldn't *you* be upset if a friend of yours was accused of murder and was hiding somewhere? What do you mean, why am I so upset? What do you want me to do, sing Christmas carols?'

'Don't shout. It's just that I never realized he meant so much to you.'

'He was a nice man,' I said, finally. 'I just hate to see him in trouble.'

She came to me and put her hand lightly on my arm. 'We'll leave this city soon, David. You won't have to think about it any more. People get into trouble, David. But don't act as though it were, somehow, your fault. It's not your fault.'

'*I* know it's not my fault!' But my voice, and Hella's eyes, astounded me into silence. I felt, with terror, that I was about to cry.

Giovanni stayed at large nearly a week. As I watched, from Hella's window, each night creeping over Paris, I thought of Giovanni somewhere outside, perhaps under one of those bridges, frightened and cold and not knowing where to go. I wondered if he had, perhaps, found friends to hide him – it was astonishing that in so small and policed a city he should prove so hard to find. I feared, sometimes, that he might come to find me – to beg me to help him, or to kill me. Then I thought that he probably considered it beneath him to ask me for help; he, no doubt, felt by now that I was not worth killing. I looked to Hella for help. I tried to bury each night, in her, all my guilt and terror. The need to act was like a fever in me, the only act possible was the act of love.

He was finally caught, very early one morning, in a barge tied up along the river. Newspaper speculation had already placed him in Argentina, so it was a great shock to discover that he had got no farther than the Seine. This lack, on his part, of 'dash' did nothing to endear him to the public. He was a criminal, Giovanni, of the dullest kind, a bungler; robbery, for example, had been insisted on as the motive for Guillaume's murder; but, though Giovanni had taken all the money Guillaume had in his pockets, he had not touched the cash-register and had not even suspected, apparently, that Guillaume had over one thousand francs hidden in another wallet at the bottom of his closet. The money he had taken from Guillaume was still in his pockets when he was caught; he had not been able to spend it. He had not eaten for two or three days and was weak and pale and unattractive. His face was on newsstands all over Paris. He looked young, bewildered, terrified, depraved; as though he could not believe that he, Giovanni, had come to this; had come to this and would go no further, his short road ending in a common knife. He seemed already to be rearing back, every inch of his flesh revolting before that icy vision. And it seemed, as it had seemed so many times, that he looked to me for help. The newsprint told the unforgiving world how Giovanni repented, cried for mercy, called on God, wept that he had not meant to do it. And told us, too, in delicious detail, *how* he had done it: but not why. Why was too black for the newsprint to carry and too deep for Giovanni to tell.

I may have been the only man in Paris who knew that he had not meant to do it, who could read *why* he had done it beneath the details printed in the newspapers. I remembered again the evening

I had found him at home and he told me how Guillaume had fired him. I heard his voice again and saw the vehemence of his body and saw his tears. I knew his bravado, how he liked to feel himself *debrouillard*, more than equal to any challenge, and saw him swagger into Guillaume's bar. He must have felt that, having surrendered to Jacques, his apprenticeship was over, love was over, and he could do with Guillaume anything he liked. He could, indeed, have done with Guillaume anything at all – but he could not do anything about being Giovanni. Guillaume certainly knew. Jacques would have lost no time in telling him, that Giovanni was no longer with *le jeune Americain*; perhaps Guillaume had even attended one or two of Jacques' parties, armed with his own entourage; and he certainly knew, all his circle knew, that Giovanni's new freedom, his loverless state, would turn into license, into riot – it had happened to every one of them. It must have been a great evening for the bar when Giovanni swaggered in alone.

I could hear the conversation:

'*Alors, tu es revenu?*' This from Guillaume, with a seductive, sardonic, speaking look.

Giovanni sees that he does not wish to be reminded of his last, disastrous tantrum, that he wishes to be friendly. At the same moment Guillaume's face, voice, manner, smell, hit him; he is actually facing Guillaume, not conjuring him up in his mind; the smile with which he responds to Guillaume almost causes him to vomit. But Guillaume does not see this, of course, and offers Giovanni a drink.

'I thought you might need a bar-man,' Giovanni says.

'But are you looking for work? I thought your American would have bought you an oil-well in Texas by now.'

'No. My American' – he makes a gesture – 'has flown!' They both laugh.

'The Americans always fly. They are not serious,' says Guillaume.

'*C'est vrai*,' says Giovanni. He finishes his drink, looking away from Guillaume, looking dreadfully self-conscious, perhaps almost unconsciously, whistling. Guillaume, now, can hardly keep his eyes off him, or control his hands.

'Come back, later, at closing, and we will talk about this job,' he says at last.

And Giovanni nods and leaves. I can imagine him, then, finding some of his street-cronies, drinking with them, and laughing, stiffening up his courage as the hours tick by. He is dying for someone to tell him not to go back to Guillaume, not to let Guillaume touch him. But his friends tell him how rich Guillaume is, how he is a silly old queen, how much he can get out of Guillaume if he will only be smart.

No one appears on the boulevards to speak to him, to save him. He feels that he is dying.

Then the hour comes when he must go back to Guillaume's bar. He walks there alone. He stands outside awhile. He wants to turn away, to run away. But there is no place to run. He looks up the long, dark, curving street as though he were looking for someone. But there is no one there. He goes into the bar. Guillaume sees him at once and discreetly motions him upstairs. He climbs the stairs. His legs are weak. He finds himself in Guillaume's rooms, surrounded by Guillaume's silks, colors, perfumes, staring at Guillaume's bed.

Then Guillaume enters and Giovanni tries to smile. They have a drink. Guillaume is precipitate, flabby, and moist, and with each touch of his hand, Giovanni shrinks further and more furiously away. Guillaume disappears to change his clothes and comes back in his theatrical dressing gown. He wants Giovanni to undress . . .

Perhaps at this moment Giovanni realizes that he cannot go through with it, that his will cannot carry him through. He remembers the job. He tries to talk, to be practical, to be reasonable, but of course, it is too late, Guillaume seems to surround him like the sea itself. And I think that Giovanni, tortured into a state like madness, feels himself going under, is overcome, and Guillaume has his will. I think if this had not happened, Giovanni would not have killed him.

For, with his pleasure taken, and while Giovanni still lies suffocating, Guillaume becomes a business man once more and, walking up and down, gives excellent reasons why Giovanni cannot work for him any more. Beneath whatever reasons Guillaume invents the real one lies hidden and they both, dimly, in their different fashions, see it: Giovanni, like a falling movie star, has lost his drawing power. Everything is known about him, his secrecy has been discovered. Giovanni certainly feels this and the rage which has been building in him for many months begins to be swollen now with the memory of Guillaume's hands and mouth. He stares at Guillaume in silence for a moment and then begins to shout. And Guillaume answers him. With every word exchanged Giovanni's head begins to roar and a blackness comes and goes before his eyes. And Guillaume is in seventh heaven and begins to prance about the room – he has scarcely ever gotten so much for so little before. He plays this scene for all its worth, deeply rejoicing in the fact that Giovanni's face grows scarlet, and his voice thick, watching, with pure delight, the bone-hard muscles in his neck. And he says something, for he thinks the tables have been turned; he says something, one phrase, one insult, one mockery too many; and in a split-second, in his own shocked silence, in Giovanni's eyes, he realizes that he has unleashed something he cannot turn back.

Giovanni certainly did not mean to do it. But he grabbed him, he struck him. And with that touch, and with each blow, the intolerable weight at the bottom of his heart began to lift: now it was Giovanni's turn to be delighted. The room was overturned, the fabrics were shredded, the odor of perfume was thick. Guillaume struggled to get out of the room, but Giovanni followed him everywhere: now it was Guillaume's turn to be surrounded. And perhaps at the very moment Guillaume thought he had broken free, when he had reached the door perhaps, Giovanni lunged after him and caught him by the sash of the dressing gown and wrapped the sash around his neck. Then he simply held on, sobbing, becoming lighter every moment as Guillaume grew heavier, tightening the sash and cursing. Then Guillaume fell. And Giovanni fell – back into the room, the streets, the world, in the presence and the shadow of death.

*

By the time we found this great house it was clear that I had no right to come here. By the time we found it, I did not even want to see it. But by this time, also, there was nothing else to do. There was nothing else I wanted to do. I thought, it is true, of remaining in Paris in order to be close to the trial, perhaps to visit him in prison. But I knew there was no reason to do this. Jacques, who was in constant touch with Giovanni's lawyer, and in constant touch with me, had seen Giovanni once. He told me what I knew already, that there was nothing I, or anyone, could do for Giovanni any more.

Perhaps he wanted to die. He pleaded guilty, with robbery as the motive. The circumstances under which Guillaume had fired him received great play in the press. And, from the press, one received the impression that Guillaume had been a good-hearted, a perhaps somewhat erratic philanthropist who had had the bad judgment to befriend the hardened and ungrateful adventurer, Giovanni. Then the case drifted downward from the headlines. Giovanni was taken to prison to await trial.

And Hella and I came here. I may have thought – I am sure I thought, in the beginning – that, though I could do nothing for Giovanni, I might, perhaps, be able to do something for Hella. I must have hoped that there would be something Hella could do for me. And this might have been possible if the days had not dragged by, for me, like days in prison. I could not get Giovanni out of my mind, I was at the mercy of the bulletins which sporadically arrived from Jacques. All that I remember of the autumn is waiting for Giovanni to come to trial. Then, at last, he came to trial, was found guilty, and placed under sentence of death. All winter long I counted the days. And the nightmare of this house began.

Much has been written of love turning to hatred, of the heart growing cold with the death of love. It is a remarkable process. It is far more terrible than anything I have ever read about it, more terrible than anything I will ever be able to say.

I don't know, now, when I first looked at Hella and found her stale, found her body uninteresting, her presence grating. It seemed to happen all at once – I suppose that only means that it had been happening for a long time. I trace it to something as fleeting as the tip of her breast lightly touching my forearm as she leaned over me to serve my supper. I felt my flesh recoil. Her underclothes, drying in the bathroom, which I had often thought of as smelling even rather improbably sweet and as being washed much too often, now began to seem unaesthetic and unclean. A body which had to be covered with such crazy, catty-cornered bits of stuff began to seem grotesque. I sometimes watched her naked body move and wished that it were harder and firmer, I was fantastically intimidated by her breasts, and when I entered her I began to feel that I would never get out alive. All that had once delighted me seemed to have turned sour on my stomach.

I think – I think that I have never been more frightened in my life. When my fingers began, involuntarily, to loose their hold on Hella, I realized that I was dangling from a high place and that I had been clinging to her for my very life. With each moment, as my fingers slipped, I felt the roaring air beneath me and felt everything in me bitterly contracting, crawling furiously upward against that long fall.

I thought that it was only, perhaps, that we were alone too much and so, for a while, we were always going out. We made expeditions to Nice and Monte Carlo and Cannes and Antibes. But we were not rich and the south of France, in the wintertime, is a playground for the rich. Hella and I went to a lot of movies, and found ourselves, very often, sitting in empty, fifth-rate bars. We walked a lot, in silence. We no longer seemed to see things to point out to each other. We drank too much, especially me. Hella, who had been so brown and confident and glowing on her return from Spain, began to lose all this, she began to be pale and watchful and uncertain. She ceased to ask me what the matter was, for it was borne in on her that I either did not know, or would not say. She watched me. I felt her watching and it made me wary and it made me hate her. My guilt, when I looked into her closing face, was more than I could bear.

We were at the mercy of bus schedules and often found ourselves, in the wintry dawn, huddled sleepily together in a waiting room or freezing on the street-corner of some totally deserted town. We arrived home in the grey morning, crippled with weariness, and went straight to bed.

I was able, for some reason, to make love in the mornings. It may have been due to nervous exhaustion; or wandering about at night engendered in me a curious, irrepressible excitement. But it was not the same, something was gone; the astonishment, the power, and the joy were gone, the peace was gone.

I had nightmares and sometimes my own cries woke me up and sometimes my moaning made Hella shake me awake.

'I wish,' she said, one day, 'you'd tell me what it is. Tell me what it is, let me help you.'

I shook my head in bewilderment and sorrow and sighed. We were sitting in the big room, where I am standing now. She was sitting in the easy chair, under the lamp, with a book open on her lap.

'You're sweet,' I said. Then: 'It's nothing. It'll go away. It's probably just nerves.'

'It's Giovanni,' she said.

I watched her.

'Isn't it,' she asked, carefully, 'that you think you've done some- thing awful to him by leaving him in that room? I think you blame yourself for what happened to him. But, darling, nothing you could have done would have helped him. Stop torturing yourself.'

'He was so beautiful,' I said. I had not meant to say it. I felt myself beginning to shake. She watched me while I walked to the table – there was a bottle there then, as now – and poured myself a drink.

I could not stop talking, though I feared at every instant that I would say too much. Perhaps I wanted to say too much.

'I can't help feeling that I placed him in the shadow of the knife. He wanted me to stay in that room with him, he begged me to stay. I didn't tell you – we had an awful fight the night I went there, to get my things.' I paused. I sipped my drink. 'He cried.'

'He was in love with you,' said Hella. 'Why didn't you tell me that? Or didn't you know it?'

I turned away, feeling my face flame.

'It's not your fault,' she said. 'Don't you understand that? You couldn't keep him from falling in love with you. You couldn't have kept him from – from killing that awful man.'

'You don't know anything about it,' I muttered. 'You don't know anything about it.'

'I know how you feel –'

'You *don't* know how I feel.'

'David. Don't shut me out. Please don't shut me out. Let me help you.'

'Hella. Baby. I know you want to help me. But just let me be for awhile. I'll be all right.'

'You've been saying that now,' she said wearily, 'for a long time.' She looked at me steadily for awhile and then she said, 'David. Don't you think we ought to go home?'

'Go home? What for?'

'What are we staying here for? How long do you want to sit in this house, eating your heart out? And what do you think it's doing to me?' She rose and came to me. 'Please. I want to go home. I want to get married. I want to start having kids. I want us to live someplace, I want *you*. Please David. What are we marking time over here for?'

I moved away from her, quickly. At my back she stood perfectly still.

'What's the *matter*, David? What do you *want*?'

'I don't know. I don't *know*.'

'What is it you're not telling me? Why don't you tell me the truth? Tell me the *truth*!'

I turned and faced her. 'Hella – bear with me, *bear* with me – a little while.'

'I want to,' she cried, 'but where *are* you? You've gone away somewhere and I can't find you. If you'd only let me *reach* you –!'

She began to cry. I held her in my arms. I felt nothing at all.

I kissed her salty tears and murmured, murmured I don't know what. I felt her body straining, straining to meet mine and I felt my own contracting and drawing away and I knew that I had begun the long fall down. I stepped away from her. She swayed, where I had left her, like a puppet dangling from a string.

'David, please let me be a woman. I don't care what you do to me. I don't care what it costs. I'll wear my hair long, I'll give up cigarettes, I'll throw away the books.' She tried to smile; my heart turned over. 'Just let me be a woman, take me. It's what I want. It's *all* I want. I don't care about anything else.' She moved toward me. I stood perfectly still. She touched me, raising her face, with a desperate and terribly moving trust, to mine. 'Don't throw me back into the sea, David. Let me stay here with you.' Then she kissed me, watching my face. My lips were cold. I felt nothing on my lips. She kissed me again and I closed my eyes, feeling that strong chains were dragging me to fire. It seemed that my body, next to her warmth, her insistence, under her hands, would never awaken. But when it awakened, I had moved out of it. From a great height, where the air all around me was colder than ice, I watched my body in a stranger's arms.

It was that evening, or an evening very soon thereafter, that I left her sleeping in the bedroom and went, alone, to Nice.

I roamed all the bars of that glittering town and at the end of the first night, blind with alcohol and grim with lust, I climbed the stairs of a dark hotel in company with a sailor. It turned out, late the next day, that the sailor's leave was not yet ended and that the sailor had friends. We went to visit them. We stayed the night. We spent the next day together, and the next. On the final night of the sailor's leave, we stood drinking together in a crowded bar. We faced the mirror. I was very drunk. I was almost penniless. In the mirror, suddenly, I saw Hella's face. I thought for a moment that I had gone mad, and I turned. She looked very tired and drab and small.

For a long time we said nothing to each other. I felt the sailor staring at both of us.

'Hasn't she got the wrong bar?' he asked me, finally.

Hella looked at him. She smiled.

'It's not the only thing I got wrong,' she said.

Now the sailor stared at me.

'Well,' I said to Hella, 'now you know.'

'I think I've known it for a long time,' she said. She turned and started away from me. I moved to follow her. The sailor grabbed me.

'Are you – is she –?'

I nodded. His face, open-mouthed, was comical. He let me go and I passed him and, as I reached the doors, I heard his laughter.

We walked for a long time in the stone-cold streets, in silence. There seemed to be no one on the streets at all. It seemed inconceivable that the day would ever break.

'Well,' said Hella, 'I'm going home. I wish I'd never left it.'

'If I stay here much longer,' she said, later that same morning, as she packed her bag, 'I'll forget what it's like to be a woman.'

She was extremely cold, she was very bitterly handsome.

'I'm not sure any woman *can* forget that,' I said.

'There are women who have forgotten that to be a woman doesn't simply mean humiliation, doesn't simply mean bitterness. I haven't forgotten it yet,' she added, 'in spite of you. I'm not going to forget it. I'm getting out of this house, away from you, just as fast as taxis, trains, and boats will carry me.'

And in the room which had been our bedroom in the beginning of our life in this house, she moved with the desperate haste of someone about to flee – from the open suitcase on the bed, to the chest of drawers, to the closet. I stood in the doorway, watching her. I stood there the way a small boy who has wet his pants stands before his teacher. All the words I wanted to say closed my throat, like weeds, and stopped my mouth.

'I wish, anyway,' I said at last, 'that you'd believe me when I say that, if I was lying, I wasn't lying to *you*.'

She turned toward me with a terrible face. '*I* was the one you were talking to. I was the one you wanted to come with you, to this terrible house in the middle of nowhere. I was the one you said you wanted to marry.'

'I mean,' I said, 'I was lying to myself.'

'Oh,' said Hella, 'I see. That makes everything different, of course.'

'I only mean to say,' I shouted, 'that whatever I've done to hurt you, I didn't mean to do!'

'Don't shout,' said Hella. 'I'll soon be gone. Then you can shout it to those hills out there, shout it to the peasants, how guilty you are, how you love to be guilty!'

She started moving back and forth again, more slowly, from the suitcase to the chest of drawers. Her hair was damp and fell over her forehead, and her face was damp. I longed to reach out and take her in my arms and comfort her. But that would not be comfort any more, only torture, for both of us.

She did not look at me as she moved, but kept looking at the clothes she was packing, as though she were not sure they were hers.

'But I *knew*,' she said, 'I knew. This is what makes me so ashamed. I knew it every time you looked at me. I knew it every time we went to bed. If only you had told me the truth *then*. Don't you see how unjust it was to wait for *me* to find it out? To put all the burden on *me*? I had the *right* to expect to hear from you – women are always waiting for the *man* to speak. Or hadn't you heard?'

I said nothing.

'I wouldn't have had to spend all this time in this *house*. I wouldn't be wondering how in the name of God I'm going to stand that long trip back. I'd *be* home by now, dancing with some man who wanted to make me. And I'd *let* him make me, too, why not?' And she smiled bewilderedly at a crowd of nylon stockings in her hand and carefully crushed them in the suitcase.

'Perhaps *I* didn't know it then. I only knew I had to get out of Giovanni's room.'

'Well,' she said, 'you're out. And now I'm getting out. It's only poor Giovanni who's – lost his head.'

It was an ugly joke and made with the intention of wounding me; yet she couldn't quite manage the sardonic smile she tried to wear.

'I'll never understand it,' she said at last, and she raised her eyes to mine as though I could help her to understand. 'That sordid little gangster has wrecked your life. I think he's wrecked mine, too. Americans should never come to Europe,' she said, and tried to laugh and began to cry, 'it means they never can be happy again. What's the good of an American who isn't happy? Happiness was all we had.' And she fell forward into my arms, into my arms for the last time, sobbing.

'Don't believe it,' I muttered, 'don't believe it. We've got much more than that, we've always had much more than that. Only – only – it's sometimes hard to bear.'

'Oh, God, I wanted you,' she said. 'Every man I come across will make me think of you.' She tried to laugh again. 'Poor man! Poor men! Poor *me*!'

'Hella. Hella. One day, when you're happy, try to forgive me.'

She moved away. 'Ah. I don't know anything about happiness any more. I don't know anything about forgiveness. But if women are supposed to be led by men and there aren't any men to lead them, what happens then? What happens then?' She went to the closet and got her coat; dug in her handbag and found her compact and, looking into the tiny mirror, carefully dried her eyes and began to apply her lipstick. 'There's a difference between little boys and little girls, just like they say in those little blue books. Little girls want little boys. But little boys –!' She snapped her compact shut. 'I'll never again, as long as I live, know *what* they want. And now I know they'll never tell me. I don't think they know how.' She ran her fingers through her hair, brushing it back from her forehead, and now, with the lipstick, and in the heavy, black coat, she looked, again, cold, brilliant, and bitterly helpless, a terrifying woman. 'Mix me a drink,' she said, 'we can drink to old times' sake before the taxi comes. No, I don't want you to come to the station with me. I wish I could drink all the way to Paris and all the way across that criminal ocean.'

We drank in silence, waiting to hear the sound of tires on gravel. Then we heard it, saw the lights, and the driver began honking his horn. Hella put down her drink and wrapped her coat around her and started for the door. I picked up her bags and followed. The driver and I arranged the baggage in the car; all the time I was trying to think of some last thing to say to Hella, something to help wipe away the bitterness. But I could not think of anything. She said nothing to me. She stood very erect beneath the dark, winter sky, looking far out. And when all was ready, I turned to her.

'Are you sure you wouldn't like me to come with you as far as the station, Hella?'

She looked at me, and held out her hand.

'Good-bye, David.'

I took her hand. It was cold and dry, like her lips.

'Good-bye, Hella.'

She got into the taxi. I watched it back down the drive, onto the road. I waved one last time, but Hella did not wave back.

Outside my window the horizon begins to lighten, turning the grey sky a purplish blue.

I have packed my bags and I have cleaned the house. The keys to the house are on the table before me. I have only to change my clothes. When the horizon has become a little lighter the bus which will take me to town, to the station, to the train which will take me to Paris, will appear at the bend of the highway. Still, I cannot move.

On the table, also, is a small, blue envelope, the note from Jacques informing me of the date of Giovanni's execution.

I pour myself a very little drink, watching, in the window pane, my reflection, which steadily becomes more faint. I seem to be fading away before my eyes – this fancy amuses me, and I laugh to myself.

It should be now that gates are opening before Giovanni and clanging shut behind him, never, for him, to be opened or shut any more. Or perhaps it is already over. Perhaps it is only beginning. Perhaps he still sits in his cell, watching, with me, the arrival of the morning. Perhaps now there are whispers at the end of the corridor, three heavy men in black taking off their shoes, one of them holding the ring of keys, all of the prison silent, waiting, charged with dread. Three tiers down, the activity on the stone floor has become silent, is suspended, someone lights a cigarette. Will he die alone? I do not know if death, in this country, is a solitary or a mass-produced affair. And what will he say to the priest?

Take off your clothes, something tells me, *it's getting late.*

I walk into the bedroom where the clothes I will wear are lying on the bed and my bag lies open and ready. I begin to undress. There is a mirror in this room, a large mirror. I am terribly aware of the mirror.

Giovanni's face swings before me like an unexpected lantern on a dark, dark night. His eyes – his eyes, they glow like a tiger's eyes, they stare straight out, watching the approach of his last enemy, the hair of his flesh stands up. I cannot read what is in his eyes: if it is terror, then I have never seen terror, if it is anguish, then anguish has never laid hands on me. Now they approach, now the key turns in the lock, now they have him. He cries out, once. They look at him from far away. They pull him to the door of his cell, the corridor stretches before him like the graveyard of his past, the prison spins around him. Perhaps he begins to moan, perhaps he makes no sound. The journey begins. Or, perhaps, when he cries out, he does not stop crying, perhaps his voice is crying now, in all that stone and iron. I see his legs buckle, his thighs jelly, the buttocks quiver, the secret hammer there begins to knock. He is sweating, or he is dry. They drag him, or he walks. Their grip is terrible, his arms are not his own any more.

Down that long corridor, down those metal stairs, into the heart of the prison and out of it, into the office of the priest. He kneels. A candle burns, the Virgin watches him.

Mary, blessed mother of God.

My own hands are clammy, my body is dull and white and dry. I see it in the mirror, out of the corner of my eye.

Mary, blessed mother of God.

He kisses the cross and clings to it. The priest gently lifts the cross away. Then they lift Giovanni. The journey begins. They move off, toward another door. He moans. He wants to spit, but his mouth is dry. He cannot ask that they let him pause for a moment to urinate – all that, in a moment, will take care of itself. He knows that beyond the door which comes so deliberately closer, the knife is waiting. That door is the gateway he has sought so long out of this dirty world, this dirty body.

It's getting late.

The body in the mirror forces me to turn and face it. And I look at my body, which is under sentence of death. It is lean, hard, and cold, the incarnation of a mystery. And I do not know what moves in this body, what this body is searching. It is trapped in my mirror as it is trapped in time and it hurries toward revelation.

When I was a child, I spake as a child, I understood as a child, I thought as a child: but when I became a man, I put away childish things.

I long to make this prophecy come true. I long to crack that mirror and be free. I look at my sex, my troubling sex, and wonder how it can be redeemed, how I can save it from the knife. The journey to the grave is already begun, the journey to corruption is, always, already, half over. Yet, the key to my salvation, which cannot save my body, is hidden in my flesh.

Then the door is before him. There is darkness all around him, there is silence in him. Then the door opens and he stands alone, the whole world falling away from him. And the brief corner of the sky seems to be shrieking, though he does not hear a sound. Then the earth tilts, he is thrown forward on his face in darkness, and his journey begins.

I move at last from the mirror and begin to cover that nakedness which I must hold sacred, though it be never so vile, which must be scoured perpetually with the salt of my life. I must believe, I must believe, that the heavy grace of God, which has brought me to this place, is all that can carry me out of it.

And at last I step out into the morning and I lock the door behind me. I cross the road and drop the keys into the old lady's mailbox. And I look up the road, where a few people stand, men and women, waiting for the morning bus. They are very vivid beneath the awakening sky, and the horizon beyond them is beginning to flame. The morning weighs on my shoulders with the dreadful weight of hope and I take the blue envelope which Jacques has sent me and tear it slowly into many pieces, watching them dance in the wind, watching the wind carry them away. Yet as I turn and begin walking toward the waiting people, the wind blows some of them back on me.

THE STORY OF PENGUIN CLASSICS

Before 1946 ...'Classics' are mainly the domain of academics and students, without readable editions for everyone else. This all changes when a little-known classicist, E. V. Rieu, presents Penguin founder Allen Lane with the translation of Homer's Odyssey that he has been working on and reading to his wife Nelly in his spare time.

1946 The Odyssey becomes the first Penguin Classic published, and promptly sells three million copies. Suddenly, classic books are no longer for the privileged few.

1950s Rieu, now series editor, turns to professional writers for the best modern, readable translations, including Dorothy L. Sayers's *Inferno* and Robert Graves's *The Twelve Caesars*, which revives the salacious original.

1960s 1961 sees the arrival of the Penguin Modern Classics, showcasing the best twentieth-century writers from around the world. Rieu retires in 1964, hailing the Penguin Classics list as 'the greatest educative force of the 20th century'.

1970s A new generation of translators arrives to swell the Penguin Classics ranks, and the list grows to encompass more philosophy, religion, science, history and politics.

1980s The Penguin American Library joins the Classics stable, with titles such as *The Last of the Mohicans* safeguarded. Penguin Classics now offers the most comprehensive library of world literature available.

1990s Penguin Popular Classics are launched, offering readers budget editions of the greatest works of literature. Penguin Audiobooks brings the classics to a listening audience for the first time, and in 1999 the launch of the Penguin Classics website takes them online to an ever larger global readership.

The 21st Century Penguin Classics are rejacketed for the first time in nearly twenty years. This world famous series now consists of more than 1,300 titles, making the widest range of the best books ever written available to millions – and constantly redefining the meaning of what makes a 'classic'.

The Odyssey continues ...

The best books ever written

PENGUIN ⊛ CLASSICS

SINCE 1946